Lick of Fire 3

Phoenix
and the
Dragon

BIANCA D'ARC

This book is a work of fiction. The names, characters, places, and incidents are products of the writer's imagination or have been used fictitiously and are not to be construed as real. Any resemblance to persons, living or dead, actual events, locale or organizations is entirely coincidental.

No part of this book may be used or reproduced in any manner whatsoever without written permission, except in the case of brief quotations embodied in critical articles and reviews.

Paul is a dragon shifter—the only one of his kind. He's been searching the world over for signs of other dragons, but so far, he's the only one. When he feels a familiar fire magic tugging him toward the Southwestern United States, he has to investigate.

Syd is very much afraid she's losing her mind. Subject to increasingly disturbing visions, she's afraid the simple premonitions she's had all her life are evolving into something darker. Something scary.

When her car breaks down in the middle of the desert, Paul appears out of nowhere to help her get back on the road again. She offers him a ride, *knowing*—somehow—that the simple gesture will change her life forever. Whether for good or evil... well... that remains to be seen.

AUTHOR'S NOTE & DEDICATION

Note: The phoenix trilogy is an offshoot of my *Tales of the Were* series, which has many nooks and crannies. This set fits after the *Redstone Clan* and overlaps a bit with the latter part of *Grizzly Cove* and the *Grizzly Cove Crossroads* set. The phoenix books (there are three of them) can be read as a standalone set or in conjunction with any of my other paranormals, since they all take place in the same basic world, just in different parts of it. Characters do crossover and make cameo appearances from time to time. For a complete rundown of all my books check the list at the end of this book or you can always check my website at WWW.BIACADARC.COM, which will always have the most up-to-date book list.

I'd like to dedicate this book to my late mother, who never read any of my books, but supported my dream with all her heart.

I'd also like to send special thanks to my editor, Jess. She's been my editor from the first book I ever had published and I'm blessed to still be able to work with her now, more than a dozen years—and many books—later.

PROLOGUE

In the town of Grizzly Cove, on the coast of Washington State, a dragon stirred. Something was going on to the south. Something very odd, indeed. Something he needed to investigate...

In the Superstition Mountains near Phoenix, Arizona, a rumble flowed through the earth, down into a secret cavern where beings of magic and myth slumbered...but not for much longer...

And, on the outskirts of the city of Phoenix, a woman clutched her head and squinted into the sun, seeing things that weren't there. Not yet, anyway. They were portents. Images out of a dream...or a nightmare. Fire in the sky, wings and bolts of flame. Showers of sparks. And evil. Unspeakable evil...

CHAPTER 1

Syd—short for her much-despised proper name, Sybil—shook her head in the parking lot of the grocery store she liked on the eastern edge of Scottsdale, Arizona. She'd had one of her dizzy spells again, but this time, the images flashing through her mind had lingered. The fear they evoked had threatened to make her scream.

She glanced around quickly. Nobody was looking at her. Nobody had seemed to notice her momentary visit to the land of space cadets. Thank goodness!

She quickly shut the hatchback of her little car and raced around to the driver's side after rolling the empty carriage to the cart return located conveniently next to her parking space. She'd parked there on purpose, just for that reason. It came in handy, now, so she could make a quick getaway.

She had a trunk full of supplies for the old man who lived out in the middle of nowhere. She brought him groceries about once a month, worried that the old dear wouldn't have enough to eat if nobody else took pity on him. He didn't have a vehicle and probably could no longer see well enough to drive anyway. As a result, he depended on friends and neighbors to keep him supplied with the things he needed.

Syd had crossed his path a few years back, when she'd been lost out there, her plans for an adventurous little day trip into the hills having taken a seriously wrong turn. Arthur had helped get her back to the highway, but not before charming her totally. He'd invited her in out of the sun and given her cold lemonade from his ancient refrigerator. They'd talked, and she realized the old gentleman was lonely for company.

She couldn't rush out on him. Instead, she stayed and listened to his stories about living out in the desert and the strange things he'd seen. Whenever she visited, he always had lemonade and stories to tell, and she ended up staying for a couple of hours, helping him put the groceries away and making sure he was well supplied with everything he needed for a couple of weeks. She even cooked for him, making lasagna or one of her few other "specialties" and freezing portion-sized amounts that he could take out later and just reheat.

Today, she'd given herself the whole afternoon to hang out with Arthur. His home was far out on a small side road that led up into the mountains. As long as she headed home before dark, she wouldn't have any problem finding the highway again, and once on the main roads, she'd be safe enough getting back to the city.

As she drove, she wondered if she could ask old Arthur about her strange visions. He was Native American and had once told her that he'd served as a shaman in his younger days. Now, he called himself a caretaker, but he'd never elaborated about what he was taking care of. She assumed it was something spiritual, like he was looking out for the planet or something, but she'd never dared to ask.

Still, he was really the only person she knew who had ever talked with any authority about non-traditional spiritual matters. Maybe he would understand about the weird things that had been happening to her and the strange visions she'd been having. She might feel foolish asking, but she decided to at least try to feel him out on the subject before she left his house.

As it turned out, Arthur was more than receptive when

Syd finally found the courage to broach the subject with him later in the day. She'd put away the groceries she'd bought for him with his help, then sat with him and drank lemonade while they talked. Eventually, she worked her way around to the subject of visions and waking dreams, which made Arthur regarded her with keen interest in his dark eyes.

"Do you have the gift?" he asked bluntly, looking at her as if measuring her in ways she couldn't quite comprehend.

"I don't know. I'm not sure what's happening to me. All I know is that it's getting more intense." She went ahead and told him about the episode in the parking lot of the grocery store, and he listened calmly, seeming to take it all in without judgment.

"What were the images? What do you remember specifically about the vision?" he asked, sitting a little forward in his chair.

She hesitated but realized she trusted him—and there really wasn't anybody else she knew with whom she could talk about this kind of thing. She took a deep breath for courage, then spoke the words that felt like crossing a line in the sand. Once she said this out loud, there would be no going back. Or, at least, that's what it felt like.

Weird.

"I was flying. Or…it felt that way. Big things were flying around me. Creatures that breathed fire. That were made of fire. Wings of fire and dark-winged things with fiery breath. At first, I thought the flying things were fighting each other, but then, I realized there was something else. Something evil below. The flames were all directed at it, but I couldn't see it clearly. Just a huge ball of flame that didn't look like any normal flames I've ever seen before."

"Two different kinds of flying creatures?" Arthur asked quietly once she'd subsided. He wasn't rushing her, which was good. She was barely able to speak the words. It all seemed so insane.

She nodded in answer to his question. "Things that were made of flame with fiery wings. And dark things with leathery

4

wings and sparkling scales that breathed fire. It was night. The whole thing was set against a dark sky, and with all the flashes of flame, I couldn't see it too well."

"My dear Syd," Arthur said slowly. "You are seeing thunderbirds." Her heart skipped a beat. "And dragons."

*

Paul wasn't sure what drew him southward, but there was some kind of familiar magic down there, calling to him. A fiery magic that spoke to his innermost being—the dragon that lived within.

He was young for a dragon. Young for a human, too. He was only in his twenties, but he'd seen more than his fair share of suffering, cruelty, and warfare. Having discovered his dragon spirit in his teens gave him the freedom to go wherever he wanted, whenever he wanted, for the most part. He had to be somewhat cautious to only fly at night or with cloud cover.

He didn't think he showed up on anyone's radar. His scales might have something to do with that, reflecting any signals that might come his way. Whatever the reason, he'd never had any indication that ground-based systems were able to see him.

He'd spent time in Canada, looking for information about others of his kind, but so far, he was the only dragon he knew about. That couldn't be right, though. Could it? He had to have come from somewhere. Although he'd grown up in an orphanage, he had to have had parents. A mother. A father. Someone. The dragon part of his heritage couldn't have just appeared out of nowhere. It didn't make sense.

He had spent time among shifters of various kinds, learning all he could about werewolves, werebears, big cat shifters and the like. As far as he'd been able to discover, they were all born that way, except in very rare cases. So, it stood to reason Paul's inner dragon had been there since birth. He had to have inherited his shifter genes from at least one of his parents, but he had no information about either one of them. As far as the orphanage records went, he had just appeared on a doorstep one night with no indication of where he had come from.

Just recently, he had connected with a bear shifter who claimed to have dragon blood in his ancestry. The bear's new mate—a *strega*, which was a kind of hereditary Italian witch—had been looking specifically for a dragon and had sought Paul out through the werewolf Pack he'd been living near in Canada. Intrigued by the situation in a strange new town called Grizzly Cove on the Washington coast that was inhabited mostly by bear shifters, Paul had flown down to check it out.

It was there he had found the bear shifter with dragon blood, and the man's grandmother—his *babushka*, whom everyone in Grizzly Cove called Granny Ivana—from the Kamchatka Peninsula on the easternmost coast of Russia, near Siberia. The old bear-woman's grandfather had been a dragon shifter of Italian origin, and she seemed to think Paul might be related to her grandfather's sister. She had put calls in to her Clan in Kamchatka, but they had still been waiting to hear what had been found in the family archives when Paul had felt the fiery magic rumbling to the south.

He'd decided to make his home—at least temporarily—in Grizzly Cove, to learn what he could from Granny Ivana. He'd told her where he was going and why when he left. He wasn't sure how long it was going to take to discover what was going on in the desert to the south, but for a dragon, it was only a short flight.

He'd left at dusk, and within an hour, he was coasting down along the tops of different mountain ranges. He could clearly see much drier lands ahead of him. He could scent the desert winds. The cactus and sagebrush. The unique plants and grit of the American Southwest. A place he had never been before but found intriguing now that he was drawing near.

Little winding roads led from the arid mountains toward

the bright lights of a sprawling city in the distance. Phoenix, he thought it was called. An intriguing name, given the mythology linking his kind with those mythical birds of flame. He wondered, for perhaps the thousandth time, if there was anything to the ancient legends.

His gaze fell on the headlights of one intrepid little car making its way through the foothills, heading toward the city. The little car was right below him as he circled, dropping altitude. He was cloaked in darkness and wanted to get closer to the ground before approaching the city. He planned to circle it several times before making a decision about where to land, or indeed, if he should land at all.

He tried to calm his mind and listen to the wind. Something had drawn him here, but he wasn't able to pinpoint the location of whatever it was that had called to him. The only thing drawing his attention at the moment was the little car—with its flickering headlights.

That didn't look good.

*

Syd started her long drive back to the city much later than she'd intended. Arthur hadn't laughed at her talk of visions. In fact, he'd gone to his bookshelf and taken down a heavy volume all about mythological creatures and showed her images that sent chills down her spine.

The artistic renderings of scaled dragons with leathery wings that breathed fire in long streams were just like in her visions. And there were thunderbirds, and firebirds, and even phoenixes, that were depicted more stylistically than what she'd seen but were still possible suspects for the creatures in her visions. She had been speechless as she looked at the pages in the book.

Arthur had given her time and space to peruse the book. He'd gone into the kitchen, ostensibly to get refills for their glasses of lemonade. She knew, however, that he'd been being polite. Her emotions were all over the place as she looked at those images, and she could even remember a tear flowing down her cheek at one point. That's probably what had sent the old gentleman scurrying for the safety of the kitchen. She chuckled, recalling those moments, even as she squinted to try to see the road ahead.

There were no streetlights this far out from the city. The road was narrow, and it would be all too easy to drive off the side of it into the sandy dirt, which was something she definitely didn't want to do at any time—especially in the dark.

Arthur had really listened to her about the visions and made her feel better. Someone believed her—and didn't think she was crazy. It was a reassurance she needed right now, even if it was only from an old codger who lived out in the middle of nowhere.

Arthur might be a bit of a recluse, but she respected him and his lifetime of experience. He had knowledge. He knew things about the world and the creatures in it. Things she didn't really comprehend but, somehow, was just beginning to understand. She trusted her instincts, which said there was a great deal more to Arthur than met the eye.

Part of it might be that he was Native American. She'd always had a deep respect for the various Native American cultures and beliefs. She loved the art and style of the Native peoples and had often wondered if there was Native blood in her heritage. She had been adopted as a baby, so she didn't know for sure, though she was really tempted to have one of those DNA tests done that would at least tell her what her cultural heritage might be.

Regardless, Arthur was a mysterious fellow who commanded her respect, though she supposed he seemed pretty harmless to most other people. Only Syd suspected the core of steel—the heart of the warrior that still beat in his elderly chest. She'd met him the one time and then couldn't get him out of her head. Going back to see him again with a trunk full of groceries had been an impulsive move, but it was something she was glad she had done.

He had to be lonely all the way out here on his own, but he wouldn't consider moving the few times she'd mentioned the nice retirement communities going up closer to the city and all their amenities. No, Arthur was happy where he was, although always glad to see her when she visited.

Today, they had talked of visions and mythological creatures. There was never a lack of conversation when they were together, but today's was especially far-reaching. She felt so much more settled now that he'd taken her seriously. The only problem was going home so late. The road wasn't the greatest even during the day, but now...

She felt almost like something was watching her progress through the dark night in the middle of nowhere. A shiver coursed down her spine, despite the heat. The desert got cold at night, though it wasn't late enough yet to be truly chilly. Still, there was a presence, of sorts, in the night. She could feel it.

And then...her headlights began to flicker.

Shit!

She'd seen this before. Her old car liked to conk out on her at various times. She could never predict where or when, but the old jalopy wasn't exactly reliable. Which was why she usually tried to stick to safe routes, and not be anywhere near no man's land at night—and she was now.

Darnit.

Although she prayed really hard to whatever gods might be listening, her little car sputtered a few times then rolled to a halt as conking noises came out of the tailpipe, finally dissipating into a rude sound.

Great. Just great.

CHAPTER 2

The car far below rolled to a stop, the electricity to the feeble headlights cutting out altogether. The dragon could see there was no one around for miles and miles as he circled lower to investigate. His wings made no sound, stretched out to slow his speed and tilted to allow him to spiral downward as gravity won out over the air currents in a measured battle he controlled.

He saw a figure get out of the compact car and walk around to the hood. He could tell as he flew ever lower that the driver was female…and all alone. What was she thinking, driving out in the desolate mountains all alone at night in a clunker of a car?

Knowing he couldn't leave her like that, he looked around for a good place to land and shift, far enough away to avoid detection and close enough to get to her in a reasonable amount of time. He decided to approach from the direction she'd been heading, so as to avoid any questions she might have about where he'd come from. If she'd been on the road for any length of time, she'd probably wonder why she hadn't noticed a man walking along it as she passed him.

Paul set down and shifted quickly, grateful once again that the extra magical power of the dragon allowed him to retain his clothing and possessions even while in shifted form. They simply went *somewhere* else—where, exactly, he didn't know—then came back when he resumed his human form. Right now, that left him wearing jeans and a white T-shirt with a backpack full of supplies he'd packed just before leaving Grizzly Cove a couple of hours before. Wearing his favorite dusty boots, he looked like a hiker. Or so he hoped. He didn't want to scare the woman. Only to help her.

"Hello?" he called as he approached. He didn't want to startle her too badly, appearing out of the dark. He clicked on a small flashlight that had been in the side pocket of his backpack.

The woman straightened from her perusal of the engine and turned sharply. "Hello?" she called back, her gaze zeroing in on the little light in his hand that he held shining on the road in front of him, even though he didn't need it to see clearly. Dragons—even in human form—had superb night vision.

"Looks like you're stuck. Can I help?"

Paul knew his words would sound accented to her. He had grown up in Romania, and English wasn't exactly his first, or even second, language. That might help him in this case, though. He decided to pose as an eccentric foreign sightseer, backpacking his way across the United States.

"Do you know anything about engines?" she called back, squinting, clearly unable to see him yet.

"A little," he replied, grateful that she seemed to be welcoming rather than fearful. Too trusting, he thought privately, but good in this case, for him. "Let me see if I can help." He closed the gap between them and took a position next to her—though not too close—in front of the engine. "I'm Paul, by the way."

"Syd," she replied quietly.

Close now, he could scent her nervousness. So. She wasn't as unaffected by the situation as he'd thought. It was good that she was cautious. A woman alone on a deserted road was not a safe thing to be in any country. There were too many predators out there that wouldn't hesitate to do such a woman harm.

But Paul was not one of them. He was a predator, of course, but he would not harm this woman. He would help her on her way and go about his business.

"I am used to European cars, but I think this one suffers from an electrical problem," he said after a few moments studying the engine. He could actually see the flow of electricity, and where it was failing. Just another one of his little quirks. He could fix her car, but he'd need a few things from his pack.

Shrugging off the backpack, he reached into the pocket where he kept a few tools and supplies. A roll of electrical tape and his Swiss Army knife was all he'd need for this repair, so he grabbed those and set to work. First, he disconnected the battery, to avoid any unnecessary shocks.

He cut a loose wire to give him a fresh connection point, then stripped the plastic sheathe off the wire, using his knife. He re-made the connection and sealed it with electrical tape before reconnecting the battery. All the while, the woman with the unlikely name of Syd watched in silence. He could tell she was lowering her alert level, little by little, as he worked without making any overt moves toward her. Good. He didn't like her being afraid of him, even if it was a healthy survival instinct in this situation.

"It should work now," he told her. "Try to start the car." He didn't close the hood. He wanted to watch the electrical flows—the path of the heat in the wires—to be sure everything was in working order before he sent her on her way.

She got into the driver's seat and turned the key. The car started, and the headlights came on with nary a flicker. Paul watched the engine for a moment to be certain, but he was pretty sure the old car would get her back to the city with no further problems. He shut the hood and went around to say goodbye. She had rolled down her window and had a worried look on her face as she regarded him. What was distressing her, now?

He didn't like the tension in her expression, and an instinct rose in him to make that look of anxiety go away. He wasn't sure where it came from or why he was reacting so strongly to this woman, but he was a creature of fire and instinct. He had to follow where the dragon led…for it had never led him wrong.

"Can I give you a ride back to town?" she asked, her tension increasing in ways Paul didn't like.

"That's all right," he told her. Was she offering despite her better judgment? Did she feel obligated to offer because he had helped her? "I'm heading that way." He pointed down the road toward where she'd come from.

"But there's nothing there for hundreds of miles," she told him, truly worried now.

What was his best move here? Should he accept her offer and ride into the city with her? Would that alarm her more—being stuck inside the car with a stranger on a dark, deserted road for however long it took to get to the city?

"I have my gear," he told her, trying to brazen it out. He patted the strap of the backpack on his shoulder and tried to sound confident, though it was pretty obvious he couldn't have enough food or water with him to survive in this terrain by himself for any length of time.

"It won't be enough. Not for a trek across the mountains. You'll need more equipment, and there are no shops this way. All the places to buy the things you need are in town," she told him, biting her lower lip. Suddenly, he felt the urge to stop her—with his own lips. If any nibbling was to be done, he wanted to be the one doing it.

She was a very attractive woman, with lush curves and a sense of latent power hidden deep inside her. Now, that was interesting.

He looked back down the road from the direction he'd come and shook his head as if coming to a decision. He would accept the ride and set her mind at ease as much as he could. He wanted to know more about this mysterious woman.

"I suppose one more night in civilization won't hurt," he told her, keeping up the pretense that he'd come from the city on his way into the mountains.

Syd was torn. The man had appeared out of nowhere to help her. She still wasn't sure about his intent, but he'd been nothing but polite and helpful since walking out of the darkness to her rescue. He might still be a serial killer, of course, but she couldn't let him walk across the desert with only the supplies in his backpack. If someone else didn't come along this road—which wasn't well traveled at the best of times—then he'd be in big trouble sooner rather than later.

He was a tourist. It was obvious from his thick Russian-sounding accent. He likely didn't fully appreciate the danger he was in trying to trek across this kind of landscape without proper preparation. She couldn't, in good conscience, leave him out here. He'd helped her. Now, it was her turn to help him.

She'd be on her guard, though. He was still an unknown, but having him in her car for the drive back to civilization was preferable to leaving him to his own devices out here in the dark and then wondering if she'd issued his death sentence. Surely, she could survive the relatively short ride back into town with no major problems? She hoped.

"Hop in," she told him, trying to sound encouraging. "There's room for your pack in the back."

"Only if you're sure you don't mind. I promise you, I'm not a criminal or anything." He gave her a smile that could melt butter. What was it about foreign men that always set her drooling at the least little provocation?

But, to be honest, this man—now that she got a good look at him from the light the car was putting out—was a hunk of epic proportions. Muscular. *So* very muscular. And handsome, too, with a little trace of a beard that looked both neat and bad-boy all the way. Dark hair, dark eyes that flashed with an inner light. When he smiled, she felt magic in the air.

But that had to be her imagination running away with her.

He'd come to her rescue. Probably saved her a very uncomfortable night, at the very least. It was just a hero complex or something. Some sort of weird psychological attachment she felt because he'd rescued her.

Right?

She had to focus. He'd said something about not being a criminal. The best way to handle this whole situation, she decided, was with humor.

"Now, if you actually were a criminal, wouldn't you claim not to be?" she challenged him, hoping to keep things light. She couldn't give in to the weird attraction she was feeling. That would just be too pathetic.

"I suppose you're right," he allowed, giving her that killer smile again. "But I really am just a traveler, making my way across the country. I thought I'd look for some of those lost mines everyone claims are in the area."

"You're a prospector?" She looked at his little pack. Prospectors these days had all sorts of equipment, didn't they? This guy wasn't prepared at all. Shaking her head, she waved at him again, making a gesture that invited him into the car.

"Not really. Just a tourist with wild ideas of what might be fun to try while I'm here." His smile was disarming...and totally enticing. Damn. This Paul was really a handsome son of a gun.

As she waited for him to open the door, she had a flash of insight. A *knowing*. This man was on a dangerous path, but he was no danger to her, personally. In fact, she suddenly knew that by inviting him into her car, she was changing both of their futures...for the better.

A sense of calm, tinged with hopeful joy, filled her. She'd felt that feeling before when she'd made momentous decisions in her life. She'd always brushed it off, but in light of the weird visions she'd been having lately, she now thought maybe she'd been experiencing a subtler form of the more intense visions all along. The *knowing* was something she'd taken for granted throughout her life, though she'd always suspected it wasn't quite "normal"—whatever that meant.

Somehow, she just *knew* stuff. And right now, she *knew* she was doing the right thing. The destined thing. The needed thing.

Paul climbed in, and suddenly, the small car seemed even smaller with his large frame taking up so much space. He'd flung his pack into the backseat and then strapped himself in like a good passenger. Revving the little engine with more gusto than it really had, she set off again, carefully picking her way down the twisty mountain road.

"So, where are you from?" she asked as a conversation starter. "You sound sort of Russian, but I'm not good with all the regional differences from that part of the world."

"I grew up in Romania, but I've been traveling for a while. This is my first time in the United States," he answered easily. His voice was warm and rough, deep and masculine. It sent little shivers of awareness down her spine.

"What do you think so far?" she asked, just to keep the conversation going while she had a private meltdown at the timbre of his voice. Damn. She'd never had quite such a strong reaction just to a man's voice. He could probably make her come just by talking to her, if he had a mind to try.

Blushing at her own thoughts, Syd was thankful it was a dark night and he couldn't see her very well in the dark interior of her car. At least, she hoped he couldn't see her well. She didn't dare take her eyes off the road to look in his direction.

"The people are very helpful," he answered, a playful note in his voice. She had to chuckle at his clever reply.

"I'm glad you think so," she said, injecting a tone of modesty into her voice. Secretly, she was pleased at his compliment and quick wits. "Have you had a chance to see any of the sights?"

"Well, I saw the coast. I started my journey in the Pacific Northwest. Washington State. The redwoods are fantastic." She could hear the true enjoyment in his words and was glad for him. "Then, I came down here through the mountains, so I didn't see anything of California, though I would like to one day. I hear those southern beaches are especially beautiful."

"But the idea of finding a lost mine was just too much to resist, eh?" she teased him a bit.

"I guess," he said slowly, as if he was considering his answer. "I confess, I was drawn to the area. I guess I just like the desert climate and the mountains more than the sea. Finding a lost mine was just something fun to try. I'm not a serious prospector or anything. Just a tourist, really."

"I'm not sure if you know this, but every once in a while, people die in the mountains looking for lost treasure. The landscape here may be pretty, but it can also be quite deadly for the unprepared." She felt it only right to warn him. She didn't have a heart to let him go out into the wilderness without the right equipment. She didn't want his death on her conscience.

"Yes, thank you for the warning. I will resupply and try again. I guess I wasn't really thinking about it when I set out. I'm used to cities," he told her, and that last bit of his statement rang false in her mind.

She didn't know why, but she knew he was lying about being a city slicker. It seemed an innocuous enough statement. What did she care if he was from the city or a true outdoorsman? Perhaps he was embarrassed about his lack of preparation for a trek into the mountains. Maybe he was trying to save his masculine pride. Either way, she let it slide for now as unimportant, though she would remember the falsehood. She didn't like it when they piled up.

Finally, they were approaching the bright lights of the big city. The metro area was sprawling, but from this direction, they'd hit Scottsdale first. Rejoining the highway, they'd already passed one of the many big resorts in the area. Tourism was a big part of the business in this area, but she suspected the man in her car didn't have that kind of money necessary to get a room at one of the fancy places. Instead, she aimed her little car for a cheaper hotel she knew on the outskirts of town. She'd leave him there, knowing that he could get just about anywhere from that spot, since there was public transportation not far away.

"Do you have a map of the city?" she asked, wondering if she had chosen the right course of action.

"Sure. No problem," he told her, not really answering her question directly, but she shrugged it off. He was an adult, and judging by the look of him, he could take care of himself in the city. The mountain trails, though... That was another matter.

"There's an outfitter near the hotel I'm aiming for that will have all the different kinds of gear you might need if you still intend to go prospecting," she told him, trying to be helpful.

He just nodded and kept looking out the window as if he'd never seen the city before. She found herself pointing out various sights as they passed them, acting as a tour guide of sorts. He seemed very interested in everything she told him.

He'd easily agreed to the hotel she suggested, as if it didn't matter all that much to him. Perhaps he was going to go somewhere else as soon as she dropped him off. She tried not to worry about his fate. Did he even have enough money for a hotel? Would he end up sleeping on the streets? She had to trust that he knew what he was doing and would be all right, because the impulse to get further involved with him was strong...and dangerous.

She stopped at a traffic light as they got into town, the number of cars on the road minimal at this time of night and this far out of the city proper. She was about to turn to her passenger and say something when dizziness washed over her like a wave. Sweeping her under. Dousing her in a vision of darkness.

Sparkles of gold whizzed past her senses, and then, she was in a cavern that she somehow knew was deep below the earth. Paul was there, standing several yards away. His focus was on something in front of him. No. Not *something*. *Someone*. Only this *person*, if she could use that word in this case, was not entirely human. Her vision clouded, and she saw two images superimposed on each other. A man…and a dragon. A golden dragon with glittering golden scales and shiny, leathery wings.

As she watched Paul face off with the dragon-man, her breath caught. He was in serious danger. For, as Paul faced the golden man-dragon, other dragonish heads were popping up behind him, all over the vast cavern. There was more than one!

A honking horn blasted Syd out of the vision, and suddenly, she was back on the road just outside of Scottsdale. Damn. That had been the clearest vision she had ever experienced, and possibly the scariest. The horn sounded again behind her, and she realized the traffic light had turned green while she'd been off in Neverland.

She cleared her throat self-consciously and hit the gas. She didn't dare looked over at Paul. She wasn't sure she could prevent herself from blurting out what she had just seen, and she knew—she *knew*—she couldn't do that. This vision stuff was kooky enough to get her committed to a mental hospital if she wasn't careful. She couldn't talk about it to just anyone.

Arthur had to remain her only confidant, for now. He was far enough out of town, and a decent enough human being, that she didn't think he would betray her secrets, no matter how outlandish. Plus, he was a former shaman. A spiritual man. He hadn't thought she was crazy, and he'd tried to help her figure out what her strange visions meant.

She didn't know what Paul would make of them. She didn't know him from Adam, really. She couldn't take a chance revealing what she had seen in detail, but she resolved to try to warn him obliquely about the dangers ahead before they parted. She wasn't sure what the multitude of dragons meant. Maybe it was a sign that he would find a cavern filled with dangers. Perhaps the dragons represented problems he would face if he kept to his proposed path and went prospecting in the mountains.

Syd wasn't sure how she was going to phrase it, but she

had to at least try to get the point across that he would face difficulties—seriously dangerous difficulties—if he insisted on searching for a lost mine. Stories were plentiful about people who went into the mountains looking for gold and never came back. She really didn't want Paul to become yet another victim of gold fever.

Regardless, the vision itself kind of freaked her out. It had been so incredibly clear. She'd seen the dragons as if they were standing right in front of her. And now that she thought about it, they didn't look exactly like the pictures in the book Arthur had shown her. No, these dragons were something else, and each looked a little different from each other. Some had horns. Some had none. They were all different colors, and they had faces as individual as human faces.

It was so weird. She thought she would recognize the golden man-dragon if she saw him on the street. That's how clearly she'd seen the man's face, even superimposed over the dragon. But what did it all really mean?

"Sorry I spaced out back there," she said into the uncomfortable silence in her car. Paul hadn't said anything, but she could feel him watching her, and when she dared to glance over at him, his gaze was filled with curiosity. "It's been a long day."

"No problem," he told her easily. "I understand."

They were nearing the hotel she'd had in mind. It wasn't expensive, but it looked clean from the outside. Hopefully, he'd be okay.

"Do you have enough money?" she asked him, realizing only after the words were out of her mouth that the question was a bit rude. "I mean..." She tried to backpedal. "I owe you for fixing my car. You saved me a lot of trouble, not to mention a mechanic's bill."

"Think nothing of it," he told her magnanimously. "I could not leave you stuck there, and you have done me a good turn by giving me a ride into town. We're even."

"Are you sure?" she asked, trying one more time as she pulled up in front of the hotel.

Paul nodded. "I'm certain. Thank you. I will be fine from here."

"Just promise me you'll be careful," she said as he opened the passenger side door and put one of his long legs out, in preparation for leaving. He paused as she put her hand on his arm. "There are things—dangerous things—in those old mines and in the caverns in the mountains around here. Things you don't want to disturb. Things that could kill you."

She couldn't speak much plainer without exposing what she'd seen. She only hoped it was enough of a warning.

He looked at her for a long moment, then his gaze slipped down to where her hand still clutched at his arm. She let go, and when she looked back at him, he was frowning, his expression tinged with regret.

"I will be very careful. I promise you. Thanks for the lift, and I wish you safe travels on your path." He got out of the car and walked away without looking back. For some reason, Syd felt a little pang in her heart, watching him go, and she had to force herself not to go after him.

Finally, she put the car in gear and drove away, but she felt as if she'd left a little piece of her behind, perhaps never to return.

Paul knew something strange had occurred at that traffic light. He wasn't sure what it was, but he'd bet the woman had some sort of magic. It was hidden, but it had sparked while her eyes had glazed over at the traffic light. Something had happened.

Curiosity piqued, Paul waited for her to drive away, then he sought the first dark alley he could find and shifted shape. He jumped into the sky and gained altitude as quickly as he could, trusting to the dark night to hide him as long as he flew above the farthest reach of the city's lights far below. He easily found the car he'd been in just a few moments ago and began to follow.

CHAPTER 3

Syd drove the rest of the way home, thinking hard. She was so caught up in her thoughts that she didn't really notice the lights on in her house when she pulled up. She always left a couple of lights on, but only when she got to the door and opened it did she realize there were way more lights on than was normal.

And way more people in her house than there ought to be!

Holy shit! She was being burgled!

She came face to face with a man wearing dark clothes and holding something with wires in his hand. Something that looked vaguely electrical. He seemed as shocked as she was for a timeless moment, then he stalked forward, his eyes narrowing with intent as she tried desperately to back out of the door she'd just walked through.

Shit! Shit, shit, shit!

She stumbled out the side door and tried to run for her car, but the man was right behind her. She felt a blinding pain on the side of her head. He'd hit her! She had time to realize what was happening just before she hit the deck, unconscious.

Far above, the dragon that was Paul saw Syd run back out of her house. He also saw the man following her and the way he hit her from behind with a rock he'd picked up from the border of plants next to the driveway.

Paul held back the trumpeting roar he wanted to make. He had to be stealthy. He dropped altitude as fast as he dared and shifted on the fly to land on two feet, ready for action. By the time he made it to the side door of Syd's house, her assailant had dragged her back inside.

Paul decided to do some reconnaissance before he barreled in. He peeked in the windows and saw not just one, but a team of people, all scrambling to tidy up before they exited. The man who'd hit Syd was issuing orders, holding electrical equipment—stuff that looked like miniature surveillance gear to Paul.

Another thing caught his eye. More than a few of the people had glowing, magical tattoos. Some were on their hands. Low-level operatives, he had learned, usually carried them on their hands. But the man who had struck Syd had it on his face. A magical glyph that glowed to Paul's dragon sight.

These people were more than simple burglars. In fact, they weren't leaving with any of Syd's possessions. No, they had brought things with them—things they had installed—and were leaving them behind in Syd's house. Cameras, Paul guessed, and recording devices. Transmitters and maybe even receivers.

Damn. What had she walked into? And why were these people installing high-tech surveillance gear in Syd's house? She had seemed like a perfectly harmless human—even if she did have a touch of magic about her.

Paul had seen enough. He stepped in the open side door and put his fists on his hips, regarding the group in the living room.

"*Altor Custodis* or *Venifucus*?" he asked boldly.

Silence reigned for a moment while every eye in the house turned to look at Paul, except Syd, of course, who was still unconscious. Her attacker had placed her on her couch. Thoughtful bastard. Paul might not kill him after all.

The leader—the one who had hit Syd—stepped forward. "Does it really matter which we are?"

Paul nodded. "It certainly does. The former, I might be inclined to let pass with a warning. The latter...I will destroy."

"You and what army, buddy?" some wise ass in the back muttered but was quickly shushed to silence. Paul decided to ignore the taunt for now.

"Come now, I see the tattoos. I know you are members of one of the ancient orders. You only need to tell me which one and decide your fate."

The leader's chin came up, his lips forming a sneer. "I don't believe you. I don't believe you can see anything."

"Your left cheek. Her right hand. His left ring finger—is he married into the group?" Paul pointed as he called out the position of each tattoo. "The back of her right hand. Shall I go on?"

The defiant chin lowered a fraction. "Okay. So you can see them. But do you know what they mean?"

"Allegiance. Fealty. Rank." Paul nodded to each one in turn, ending with the leader. "I would need to study the glyphs in more detail to decipher their exact meanings, but somehow, I don't think you all want to stick around that long." Paul leaned against the doorjamb as if he had all the time in the world.

"We are *Altor Custodis*," the leader said after a long pause.

"Why are you interested in this woman?" Paul asked rapid fire.

"She has been reported to us as acting strangely the past few weeks. Perhaps a magical power awakening. Surveillance was ordered to confirm." The man stepped forward aggressively. "Who are you?"

"Nobody you want to mess with," Paul replied easily, letting just a little of the dragon into his voice. Sometimes, the dragon's voice could compel weak-minded humans.

"If you know enough to know what the *AC* is, then you know our mandate is exactly that—to observe and record

24

magical beings, of which, you are clearly one." Apparently, this human wasn't affected by the magic of Paul's voice. Pity.

"I am merely a newcomer to whom this human woman was kind. Her car broke down. I saw it and fixed it for her, so she didn't have to spend a very uncomfortable—not to mention possibly dangerous—night out in the middle of nowhere. She offered me a ride back to town. End of story." Paul tried to sound as nonchalant as possible. Under no circumstances did he want to give these people any reason to suspect Syd was anything other than the normal, garden-variety human. "I suspect you had something to do with her car malfunctioning?"

The man shrugged insolently. "A delaying tactic. No more."

"So, you would have sent a tow truck to rescue her after you were done invading her privacy here?" Paul waited a beat, but the other man didn't reply. Paul shook his head. "I thought not. That's pretty despicable behavior for a group that claims to not want to interfere but only observe and record. Your so-called *delaying tactic* could have led to her death, don't you realize that?"

"Come on," the leader finally scoffed. "I seriously doubt—"

Paul cut him off. "I can solve this easily." He popped his cell phone into his hand. It looked like magic, but it was really only sleight of hand. Still, the onlookers seemed impressed. "I can just call the police right now, and clear this whole thing up. When she wakes, she will recognize me. I seriously doubt—" Paul deliberately echoed the leader's words using the same tone, "—she'll welcome the sight of your team. Especially not you. After all, you did bash her over the head."

"Let's be reasonable about this. We placed our equipment. We'll just watch her for a few weeks to make sure she's human, then we'll leave her alone." The leader held up both hands, palms facing outward as if to calm Paul down, but he was having none of it.

Paul advanced an aggressive step into the room. "How

about this, instead? You leave and never return. You forget all about this woman…*and* me. I dismantle all your devices and destroy them, and you leave us all the fuck alone!"

Yeah, he lost his temper toward the end there, but he hated the *AC* and the way they watched every last move, yet did nothing to help in the struggle between light and dark. The one and only *AC* contact he'd had back home had flatly refused to tell Paul what he knew about his parentage. If, in fact, he really had known anything. He kept claiming that all *AC* records were strictly off limits to anyone but members of the order and, of course, only non-magical humans could be members.

It was all bullshit as far as Paul was concerned. That *AC* bastard had probably known where Paul's parents were. He just refused to share what he knew. Paul figured if the order wouldn't bend enough to help an orphan reconnect with his family, then they had no heart at all.

"That's not an option. We have a job to do here—" the leader tried to say, but Paul cut him off again.

"Answer this question, then. Do you want to live? Unlike this woman, whose home you invaded with your surveillance equipment—who you knocked into unconsciousness with no thought for her wellbeing—I'm not human. I don't live by the same rules as the rest of you. I could kill you all where you stand and not blink an eye. So, perhaps the question should be, how badly do you want to live?" Paul let them think about that for a moment. "I'm feeling charitable for, say…the next five minutes, but if you're not gone by then, I will start to feel distinctly uncharitable. Do you understand?"

To his credit, the leader stood his ground for another thirty seconds, or so, while the group behind him began to scramble. When they started to run past him toward the door, leaving whatever gear they'd been working on behind, the leader growled and joined them.

Stupid man, he turned at the threshold and pinned Paul with a hate-filled glare. "This isn't over."

"Oh, my friend, I think you will find that it is," Paul said to the empty doorway as the team scrambled down the drive to the van they'd parked in a dark patch down the street.

Paul closed and locked the door behind them, then went first to check on Syd. She was breathing steadily and just starting to come around. Paul sat on the edge of the couch and cupped her cheek, trying to gauge how hurt she really was.

"Syd? Can you hear me? How do you feel?" he asked in as gentle a tone as he could manage.

"Ow." She tried to sit up but gave up after a quick attempt and lay back down on the couch. "Somebody hit me," she whispered, managing to inject a bit of outrage into the hushed tone.

"I know. I saw it happen," Paul told her. "I'm sorry, but I followed you home. Just to make sure you were safe. As it turned out, it was a good thing I did." He looked around at the surveillance equipment, some of it left in plain sight. Some, he knew, was already installed and probably watching or listening in on their every move.

"What were those people doing in my house?" she asked groggily.

"Planting bugs. Video and audio, I suspect. Will you be all right while I take a look around? I have some experience with these kinds of things." Too much experience, he thought. The *AC* had bugged his home back in Romania many times.

Every time he had found a bug and destroyed it, it would be replaced soon thereafter. He tried moving to a different apartment in a different building, and still, his place would be bugged. He'd moved to a different town, same thing. Different cities? Same story. He hadn't been able to escape their surveillance for very long, which was why he had taken up globetrotting. Never staying in one place long enough for them to find him and start watching him all over again.

In answer to his question, Syd closed her eyes and lay back on the couch. He had no doubt she was in pain, but she was conscious, and her pupils seemed to react normally. He could do something for her pain, but he didn't want an audience to his magical abilities. As far as he knew, the *AC* didn't know exactly what he was. Oh, they may have guessed, but he'd been very careful never to confirm their suspicions, and he wouldn't start now.

Methodically, he went through each room in the house, finding multiple bugs in every room—even the bathroom. Despicable. He checked the closets, and sure enough, even there, small recording units had been secreted in a newly-made cubbies in the wall—high in the back, where Syd might never have noticed them. All the smaller units with limited range would report back to the recording units for broadcast in data packets, a few times a day.

Which meant that, in all likelihood, the people who had put these bugs in weren't watching in real-time. Of course, they had to know he was removing all their hard work, so they were probably out there somewhere right now, hitting the download button as fast as they could in order to get some footage of him. He worked faster. It was a race, of sorts, to disable everything before they could get any usable information from their half-completed installation.

He removed the power sources from every piece of equipment as he went along. The memory chips would be next. He wouldn't destroy the gear. For one thing, it was expensive stuff. Highly miniaturized. Some of it could be repurposed into a security system, if Syd wanted one. Or, if she never wanted to see the stuff again, he could easily bring it back to Grizzly Cove and give it to someone there who would know what to do with it. Paul judged he'd taken out at least a few thousand dollars' worth of gear so far, with a bit more still to go.

While he was moving around Syd's house, he couldn't help noticing things. Her possessions were light. The house looked as if she'd just moved in recently. Or maybe, she just liked the Spartan look, but somehow, he doubted it. He did find her laptop and put that aside. He'd have to spend some time examining that to see what the interlopers might've installed there to spy on her computer usage. He assumed there's be a keystroke logger, at the very least. Perhaps something even more insidious.

Once he cleared the laptop's system, he could use the machine to download the surveillance chips, then clear them to reset the individual pieces of equipment. He found a few wires that would suffice for the task and put them and the computer on the dining table, near the pile of disabled gear.

Every time he ventured back into the living room, which was part of an open-concept design where the living, dining and kitchen areas were all part of the same big space, he checked on Syd. She would rouse and ask him what time it was or for a sip of water, but then would lapse back into sleep—or unconsciousness—he wasn't sure which. She would be okay, though, until he was certain they weren't being watched. Then, he'd do a bit of magic and fix her up as best he could.

Syd became aware of someone touching her head. Paul. The handsome man who'd been in her car. He was in her house now, and she wasn't quite sure how that had happened. She felt a tingling warmth spreading from his hands to her head, and the pain and confusion lifted a bit. It still hurt, but she was able to think a little better. Then, she remembered.

"Those people," she whispered. "You made them go?"

"It's okay, Syd," he crooned to her as he let her head fall gently back onto the throw pillow. She realized she was laying on the couch in her living room. "They're gone now, and I'm removing the things they put in your house. You're safe now."

She felt him move closer and smelled the cinnamon-y scent of him as her eyes closed. And then, she thought she felt a whisper of a kiss on her forehead before sleep took her away again.

The next time she roused, she opened her eyes and immediately saw Paul sitting at her dining table, her laptop open and on in front of him. Why was he using her computer?

29

Syd sat up, her hand going to her head as it throbbed. Ow. Darnit, that other man had hit her on the head, and she was going to be feeling it for a while, she was sure. But her mind was clear. That was something, at least.

She just sat there for a few minutes, giving her head time to stop spinning a bit. She glanced over at Paul and the computer and was a little shocked to see images of her own bedroom on the screen. The image showed Paul walking into the room and looking around. He paused by her bedside lamp and removed something small with wires from under the base. He made his way around the room until seeming to recognize the camera. Then, he reached out for it, and the last image was of his hand—an ultimate close-up before the image went black.

"How are you feeling?" Paul asked, even as he unhooked some wires from a small device then plugged in another piece. Immediately, another image started playing on her laptop screen. This was a view of her living room and the strange people in it, moving through her house.

Syd rose slowly to her feet, more interested in what she saw on the screen than the pounding in her head. She walked slowly over to the table, her eyes glued to the screen.

"Those people were all over my house," she said, watching them in utter bafflement. "Why?"

"They were a team sent to install surveillance gear," Paul told her in a calm voice as he pointed to the pile of black wires and tiny plastic bits on the table. "I removed it and am downloading some of the images, so we can identify the team members, if possible. Then, I'm blanking the individual chips in each piece of the gear and resetting everything, so nobody can remotely access anything."

"What about my laptop? What if somebody steals that? Won't everything be on there now?" she asked.

Paul pointed to a USB drive sticking out the side of her laptop. "I'm saving it all to this, not your hard drive. It's far easier to keep a little USB drive safe than a laptop."

"You sound like you know what you're doing," she

observed, wondering again about him and what he was doing here, even though she didn't want to look a gift horse in the mouth. He'd saved her from those people and knew what to do about the bugs. She was grateful for that and wouldn't press him too hard. She needed his help…at least for now.

"I've done some work in electronic security back home. All this gear is made in China and Japan nowadays so it's pretty universal. We use the same stuff in Romania." He turned to look at her. "How's the head?"

"Painful, but I'm thinking clearly again. Thanks for watching over me." She took a seat next to him at the table. "How long was I out of it?"

"About an hour," he replied. "Maybe an hour and a half. I checked your pupils, and you don't seem to have a concussion, but I was standing by in case you needed help. If you didn't wake up on your own soon, I would have called in medical help."

"Thank you," she said, knowing she owed this man a great deal for the assistance he had rendered. She was going to say more when her attention was caught again by the action on the screen. She saw herself walking into her own living room from the side door that opened onto the driveway. "Damn. I blundered right into the middle of that, didn't I?" Paul moved his hand, probably intending to turn off the playback, but Syd reached out and covered his hand with hers. "No, let it play."

She watched herself run out, followed swiftly by the man who had hit her on the head. There was audio too, she realized, and she grabbed the mouse herself and turned up the volume. She saw herself being carried back in, slumped over the man's shoulder in a fireman's lift. He dumped her on her couch and started barking orders to his people to hurry up.

"He's the leader," she realized, speaking it aloud.

"Yes," Paul answered. "I believe so."

The team was bustling around, moving into high gear, and then, Paul walked in. All activity ceased as he spoke, and she watched in fascination as he confronted the leader of the group. It was clear from the words and images—and the body language—that Paul was not in league with these people.

Syd trusted her ability to hear when someone was telling a lie, and nothing she heard from Paul's side of the conversation with the team leader rang false. The other man, however...

When the leader claimed to be *Altor* something, he was lying. She heard it as plain as day. Syd clicked the pause button and turned to Paul.

"You know he was lying, right?" she asked him point blank. "He's not this *Altor* whatever. He's something else."

"How do you know?" Paul's eyes narrowed as he regarded her.

She countered with a question of her own. "How did you see the tattoos you two were talking about? I don't see anything. There are no marks on them."

Paul sat back in the chair and just looked at her for a moment. He seemed to search her gaze for something, then come to a decision.

"All right," he said on a gusty sigh, both of his hands on his thighs. "I have some magical ability. The tattoos they had were magical glyphs, only visible under certain circumstances to the vast majority of people, but visible to me at all times. I have what's known in my country as *sight*. I can literally see magic."

Syd was nonplussed. Of all the answers she might have expected, that wasn't one of them.

"That's a thing? Like a real thing?" she asked before she could stop herself. Paul seemed to find it amusing, his lips curling upward.

"Yes, Syd. It's a real thing," he told her patiently. "In my country, magic is much more widely accepted than here. Romania has an ancient culture."

"Whereas the United States is less than three centuries old. I get it," she told him, nodding. "We rely more on technology than magic here."

"Now, tell me, how do you know he was lying?" Paul seemed interested, not disbelieving.

Syd shrugged. "It's just something I've always been able to do. I know when people are lying to me."

"Really?" He looked skeptical, so she decided to prove herself.

"Like when you lied to me about being used to cities. I knew right away that wasn't true. You prefer the country, don't you?" She had never told anyone about her little lie-detecting ability before, but suddenly, it was important to her that Paul believe her.

His gaze narrowed again. "You are correct. I prefer wide-open spaces, but what I told you wasn't a complete falsehood. I grew up in a city."

"Maybe, but you said something about preferring cities. That was a lie."

Paul bowed his head slightly. "Very true. I can see I'm going to have to choose my words more carefully around you if I feel the need to tell falsehoods. That is an impressive gift you have. It must be very helpful to know when you are being lied to."

"Helpful…and isolating. You wouldn't believe how many people find it acceptable to lie all the time about silly things. I just can't be around that type of person. It drives me nuts." Her disgusted tone earned her Paul's amusement. Rather than continue the conversation, she clicked the play button on the video and watched the rest of the drama unfold.

She was incensed when she heard her car trouble described as a delaying tactic. Those bastards had not only invaded her home but had sabotaged her engine! They were the reason she might've been stranded alone on a stretch of road that seldom saw vehicular traffic.

Syd wanted to applaud when Paul threatened the call the police and the leader's face visibly paled. But when Paul threatened to kill them all… Syd frowned. He hadn't been lying. Not one little bit. Was Paul a murderer?

Then, he said he wasn't human. Not *human*? Syd turned to

look at Paul.

"What are you, if not human?" she asked, shaken.

"Have you ever heard of shapeshifters?" He countered her question with one of her own.

She frowned at him. "My friend, Arthur, is Native American. I know his culture has some stories about people who can turn into animals and back again. Is that what you are?"

"Something like that," he replied, and she could hear no falsehood in his words. "But from the other side of the world."

Just at that moment, her phone rang. Syd got up to answer it, breaking the tension in the room. She hung up after only a few moments and went back to stand by the table.

"It was a telemarketer," she told Paul unnecessarily. He'd probably figured it out already based on her part of the conversation.

"Good. Don't have any conversations on that phone until I've had a chance to check the line." He turned back to the computer and booted up another section of footage. "They say something here you should hear," he told her, before hitting the play button.

CHAPTER 4

Syd's jaw just about hit the floor when she heard the people on the team that had invaded her home mention the name of one of her coworkers. Elliot worked in the office, while Syd spent most of her time outdoors in the nursery, working with the plants and trees they nurtured for sale and eventual inclusion into the local landscape.

"That bastard!" she said, when it became clear from the talk between two of the team members who were placing bugs in her kitchen that Elliot had reported her recent strange behavior to these people.

"What happened at work that revealed you?" Paul asked in a no-nonsense voice once the recording had ended.

"I saw something fall on Lizzie and break her leg, only, when I came out of my momentary daze, it hadn't happened yet. It was about to, though. I ran over and caught a large stone statue, redirecting its path so it didn't hit her, just in the nick of time," she admitted. "And there were a couple other things like that." She didn't really want to go into detail.

"You see the future?" Paul asked point blank.

"I don't know. Maybe? I see things, but this is new. It only just started happening in the past few weeks, and it's been getting clearer and clearer, but I can't control it or anything."

"So." Paul sat back in his chair. "Something has awakened

a magical ability in you, and this Elliot person knew enough to not only recognize the signs but also who to call to put you under observation."

"Who were those people? What is that *Altor* thing you all were talking about?" She could only focus on so much at a time. The fact that Paul had claimed not to be human was something she would deal with later. As was the fact that he didn't seem at all nonplussed by speaking of magic and clairvoyance, while it still freaked her out.

"The *Altor Custodis* is an ancient order of watchers. They have kept detailed records of magical folk for centuries. Perhaps millennia. It's hard to learn much about them, because to be a member, one is supposed to be a non-magical human. They seem to think that by keeping track of all the Others in the world, they are doing some kind of service to humanity or something. Frankly, I have my doubts about their mission or their groups' purity. It may have started off well enough, but in recent decades, their databases could have been easily corrupted to isolate and destroy those of us who fight on the side of Light." He paused, taking a breath and seeming to consciously suppress some of his anger. "There have been warnings issued at the highest level in recent years that the *AC* has been infiltrated by the *Venifucus*."

"And the *Venifucus* are...?"

"Servants of evil. Magical folk who use their powers for dark purposes in service to the Destroyer of Worlds, the Mater Priori, a fey witch named Elspeth, who laid waste to this realm centuries ago. Some say, she's come back, and the *Venifucus* organized it, though I haven't seen any direct proof of that yet, only anecdotal evidence."

"She doesn't sound like a nice person," Syd said, knowing she was making quite the understatement.

"If evil has a face, it's hers." Paul's tone was flat as he seemed to suppress his deeper emotions.

"So, let me get this straight. Elliot noticed a few things that happened at work, and he either knew someone who's a member of one of these groups or is one himself. He felt strongly enough about the little incidents that I thought I had hidden pretty well that someone sabotaged my car and set up this huge operation, not to mention laying out the money for all this equipment, to watch my every move." Syd was struck again by how sinister this all seemed.

"That's about the size of that." Paul gestured toward the pile of wires and plastic in the middle of the table. "Though, we can reuse a lot of this. If not here, in a security system for your house, then I know some people who can definitely put this stuff to better use. They might even pay you for it, if you like."

"They're not like those others? They won't use it to spy on innocent people, will they?" She wanted to make sure before she agreed to anything.

Paul shook his head. "Strictly protective use. Defensive. Never offensive. I swear."

"Then, you have my blessing to just give it all to them. As far as I'm concerned, I never want to see any of it ever again."

Paul looked as if he wanted to argue—perhaps about installing some of it around her house or on the grounds—but she'd made up her mind. That equipment might be innocent in and of itself, but it would always carry negative connotations in her mind. She didn't want it around.

"So, what else can you do?" Paul hit her with the question seemingly out of left field.

"What? Like magic tricks?" She shook her head. "Sorry. I'm new to all this. I have no control over what I see, or when I see it. Even then, I usually don't understand what it is I'm seeing. Just lately, the visions all have to be some kind of weird metaphor."

"What makes you say that?" Paul's eyes narrowed as he looked at her.

"Winged things. Fire in the sky. Fiery wings and dark wings," she told him. "Arthur says they're mythological creatures. Phoenixes and dragons. But what does it all mean?"

Paul had a better idea of what her visions could mean than he really wanted to let on. He had made the statement to the supposed *AC* agents that he wasn't human, and he knew Syd wasn't just going to drop that subject. She would ask him more about it. He was sure of it. But admitting that he was a dragon wasn't something he wanted to do right now. If it came out later, so be it, but he wasn't going to advertise the exact nature of his other half when Syd was still largely an unknown, and a target of one of the ancient orders.

Whether it was the *AC* or the *Venifucus* didn't really matter. Paul didn't want to become a target for either one of them, though perhaps he had already drawn the bullseye on his own back by coming to Syd's defense tonight.

She seemed so genuinely confused about her visions that something inside him wanted to take pity on her and explain. He couldn't do it. Not in full. Perhaps, though, he could give her a partial explanation. Something that might help settle her mind and help her interpret the things she saw a little more easily.

"There are shapeshifters that fly," he told her gently. "Winged things. Eagles. Hawks. Mostly larger birds of prey."

"The things I've seen aren't exactly like birds. At least, not any kind of bird I've ever seen. The ones with feathery wings are always on fire, yet they don't seem to mind. Arthur said they might be phoenixes. The things with the scales and dark wings are *breathing* fire. Like dragons in some kind of dark fairy tale." She frowned. "It has to be some kind of metaphor, doesn't it?"

Paul knew he was making a pained face. How could he tell her this without revealing too much?

"Not...uh..." He squirmed a bit, not wanting to say this badly and fearing her reaction a bit. Would she scoff? Or would she get scared? Either was a possibility.

"What?" she challenged when he didn't go on right away.

"I was going to say, not necessarily. There are stories from the past—not that distant a past either—that say both of those now-mythological creatures once existed. And, they

38

were shapeshifters, living their lives in two forms. Human and the creatures that shared their souls."

Syd sat back in her chair. "Seriously?"

She looked so adorably confused, he wanted to reach out and kiss her. Hmm. Now, that was a thought. A strange thought to have about a woman he'd only just met by pure chance.

Or, had a really been mere luck that had drawn his attention to her car far below? Or, had the Mother of All had something to do with it? She had been poking Her divine nose in his affairs, for a while now. Paul might have a somewhat uneasy relationship with the Goddess, but he revered Her as a being of ultimate Light, and Paul served the Light—and Her—though he didn't always have the same kind of reverence toward Her as many other shapeshifters did. They probably thought of him as *irreverent*, if not downright blasphemous, but he and the Lady had come to a sort of understanding.

Maybe She had decided to push him in the right direction once again. If so, he was obliged for Her help, though on occasion, he had discovered that when She pushed him in a particular direction, it was more for Her benefit than his own. He would end up helping people that She wanted helped, whether or not they could contribute to his ongoing quest.

Paul didn't really begrudge any of those people he had helped in Her name. They were uniformly good souls, who had deserved the assistance he had rendered. If he'd come across them any other way, in all likelihood, he would have done the same thing. It was just that gentle nudge from above that sometimes annoyed him. He didn't like feeling as if he was just another tool in Her arsenal. Another agent to be set a task.

No, he had his own task. His own quest. He wanted Her help with that, but She was somewhat stingy with her help in his quest to find his parents—or others of his kind. He didn't even know if he was the only one left. In all his years of searching, he had never come across another dragon shifter.

The closest he had come was Peter and his *babushka* up in Grizzly Cove. They, at least, had dragon blood, but they were both bear shifters.

"Tell me why I saw you talking with dragons," Syd said, out of the blue, recalling Paul to their conversation.

"Wait. You saw what?" He held his breath, waiting for her answer.

"You were in a cavern. A glittering gold cavern, and there was a man, who was also a dragon. He was golden in both forms, and I saw his image superimposed, one on top of the other, both translucent. He was both dragon and man."

"A shapeshifter," Paul breathed as she met his gaze, shaking her head in wonder.

"You were talking to him, and other dragon heads popped up behind him all over this enormous cavern, as if they were waking up. Interested in what was going on. In what you were saying to each other. I thought, last night, that it was some sort of warning about going into the mountains. That you could face dangers there that might kill you, or something."

"Or, it could mean exactly what it looks like. I might find a nest of dragon shapeshifters in the mountains. But where?" Paul tried hard to hide his eagerness but knew he was probably failing. "Did you see anything to indicate where this cavern might be?"

"Are you telling me that you're seriously going to go out *looking* for a cave full of dragons?" She looked frightened, if he was any judge. He didn't know what to tell her, without revealing his own deepest secret.

"And if I said I was?" he asked instead of answering her question directly.

"Then, I'd say you were crazy. Who goes out *looking* for dragons? Don't dragons *eat* people? Do you *want* to get fried?" She sent him a disbelieving look. "What do you think they will do to you if you find them? They must be hiding in the mountains for a reason, and I bet they don't want to be disturbed."

40

"They may not wish to be disturbed, but I have been searching for them most of my life. I must seek them out," he told her. "Do you have any clues about where to look?"

Syd shook her head. "All I saw was the inside of the cavern. I have no idea where it's located or how to find it."

"But it was gold, right? So, an abandoned gold mine?" Paul asked, excited by the idea of a fresh clue in his quest. Maybe the Mother of All had done him a good turn this time, making his path cross with this particular nascent witch.

"There are rumors of abandoned gold mines all over the mountains," she told him. "Or it could be some sort of natural deposit nobody ever found. The mountains around here aren't exactly friendly to human exploration."

"Leave it to me," he told her. He wouldn't repeat his claim about not being human. No sense riling her even further.

Paul had a hard time containing his glee. Syd had just given him the first real hope he'd had in a long time. Certainly, finding Peter and his *babushka* in Grizzly Cove had been a high point, but they weren't dragons. They might be family—distant family—but their dragon blood was too diluted to allow them to shift into dragon form.

Syd had talked about seeing multiple dragons in her vision. One golden dragon—probably the leader of the nest—and several others behind him. The description of what she had seen lit a fire deep in his belly. A fire filled with hope that he might not be the only dragon shifter left on Earth. He might finally find others like him. He might finally not be all alone.

Syd's stomach picked that moment to growl. She hadn't had anything to eat since lunch, and it was well past dinnertime. She got up and went in search of her cell phone, finding it on a kitchen counter, near the landline extension. Her brow furrowed. She hadn't left it there. Which meant...

"Those bastards were doing something to my cell phone."

Paul was beside her a moment later. "I doubt they had time, but just to be safe, I wouldn't use it if I were you. We can get you a replacement tomorrow, but in the meantime, you can use mine."

She turned to him, feeling suddenly fragile. She'd held up pretty well until this moment, but she was tired and hurt, and hungry. It all just crashed in on her, and she reached out to him.

He didn't let her down. Paul took her into his arms, and for a moment, she felt safe again. As if nothing could hurt her, as long as he was here.

It was silly, really. She'd only just met the man. She shouldn't have this level of trust or comfort with him so soon, but those instincts that had never steered her wrong were insisting that he was safe. A port in a storm.

"It's okay," he told her, speaking softly, making her feel that it really was going to be okay, regardless of the turmoil her visions showed.

"I'm sorry," she said after a while, trying to move back, out of his embrace. He let her go just so far, making her meet his gaze before he'd let her go entirely.

"You have nothing to be sorry for, honey," he told her. "You're the victim here."

He held her gaze until she nodded, then he gave her a small grin that seemed to lighten her from within. He let her go, but the connection between them felt like it had been forged in iron and would never break now. He'd touched something deep inside her with his care, and she knew in her heart that, regardless of what kind of magic he carried inside him, he was a good man.

"Now, what did you want the phone for?" he asked gently, reminding her of what had brought her to this point.

"I'm hungry. How about you?" she said, reaching for a flyer she had kept on her fridge, held there by a magnet from the nursery where she worked. The paper was a menu from a local restaurant. She ordered delivery from them every once in a while. Particularly when she'd run out of groceries and didn't have time to shop.

The irony that she'd been to the grocery store only this afternoon wasn't lost on her, but those groceries had been for

Arthur. For her own supplies, she shopped in a store closer to home, so the perishables wouldn't spoil due to the hot temperatures that were common in this town.

She handed the menu to Paul. "Anything on there appeal to you?" she asked. "You'll stay for dinner, right? I mean, that's the least I can offer you for all you've done, but I don't have any supplies in the house and don't really feel like cooking anyway. So, let's order in, okay?"

Paul dipped his head in a very old-world way. "I'd be happy to join you for dinner, but I insist it be my treat." He held up one hand when she would have argued, and she gave in. Another time, she would have fought with him about it, but not tonight. She'd been through too much today.

They spent a few minutes talking over the menu and various dishes before arriving at an order, which he called in on his cell phone. While he dealt with the dinner order, she went into the bathroom and took a look at the cut on her head as best she could. It hurt like a bitch, and it was on the side where she could just about see it but not really treat it. Damn. She'd need his help again.

Not that he hadn't been really kind to her, but she hated feeling so helpless. Syd wasn't normally dependent on anyone. An orphan from an early age, she'd been on her own most of her life. She'd had foster parents, but they had been distant—mostly because she had been a prickly kid who didn't trust easily, and whenever they lied to her, she'd known. She could never fully trust people who lied to her, and without trust, the relationships had never grown.

Feeling frustrated tears gathering behind her eyes, she put both hands on the edge of the sink, just willing herself to calm down. It didn't really work. She wanted to cry, rage and scream for everything that had thrown her off balance today, but she held it all in.

That was when Paul appeared in the open doorway, his handsome face holding an understanding expression. She almost lost it then, but she held strong. She wouldn't cry. She wouldn't be weak.

"Can I help you with the head wound? It's in a tough spot, isn't it?" he asked, moving farther into the small room.

"Yeah, I can see it, but not well enough to clean it up." She let go of her death grip on the sink and sank down to sit on the lid of the closed toilet. The guest bathroom wasn't big, and Paul took up most of the space just with his presence.

He took the wet washcloth she held out and moved closer. When his hand touched her head, there was no pain. His fingers were gentle on her scalp, and he warned her when he was using the washcloth and kept up a running commentary on what he was doing and how the wound looked.

"It's just a small cut, really," he told her. "It's already scabbed over, so I don't think we should try to put a bandage on it. Maybe some of that antibiotic ointment would be a good idea, though."

She directed him to the medicine cabinet and helped him pick the proper tube. She thought about a bandage, but the cut was right in the middle of her hair. Anything adhesive would be a problem and she didn't feel like going around wrapped up in gauze like a mummy. He put the ointment on and helped her part her hair a bit differently, leaving the cut exposed, then tied it back with the hair band she'd had in her pocket.

"Now, just hold still for a moment," Paul said, raising his hand to hover just over where she'd been clobbered. His gaze was intent on the spot.

Syd frowned. She felt a tingle, and then, she *saw* something. A kind of glow going from his hand to her head. Magic. Had to be. Because, as he held his hand there, the pain subsided little by little. It still hurt, but a lot less by the time he moved his hand away.

"That's enough for now, I think. How's it feel?" he asked.

"A lot better," she told him, amazed at the casual way he'd just done that.

"All right, then," he said. "You're good to go."

Paul's gaze met hers in the mirror, and the moment froze. She should be thanking him—yet again—but she couldn't get the words out. So much had happened between them in such a short time. She felt she knew him well, even in the space of the few hours since they'd first met. He'd come to her rescue more than once, and though she'd helped him by giving him a ride, she knew he'd done way more for her in that span of hours than she had for him.

Somehow, though...it didn't matter. He wasn't keeping score. She could tell, though how she knew, she wasn't entirely sure. He was just that kind of man. He went out of his way for others and didn't expect anything in return. A kind soul.

The doorbell rang, breaking the spell.

"That'll be the food. I'll get it," Paul said, leaving her with seeming reluctance.

She was glad for the interruption. She was perilously close to losing all sense of reason around him. She had never met another man like him. He was strong, more honest than most, and had already rescued her twice. Not a bad record for only a few hours.

He was also drop dead gorgeous. There was a sort of nobility about him that she sensed in every act. It was innate. Something he'd been born with, and that would last through his whole existence.

Maybe it had something to do with the magic he claimed to have. She wasn't sure. She shouldn't really be thinking of him in these semi-romantic terms. Not until she knew what it was that was so different about him. She wanted desperately to know what it was that made him claim not to be human.

He'd hinted at being some sort of shapeshifter. Mind-blowing as that idea was, Syd found herself accepting it more easily than she would have believed just a few months ago. Of course, she hadn't been entertaining visions until recently and hadn't really thought much about magic or clairvoyance until it had started happening to her.

She heard him moving around in the main area, so she got herself together, took one last look in the mirror and headed out to join him. Her head still hurt a bit, but it was so much better than it had been before he did…whatever that was he'd done. One thing was certain, whatever kind of beast shared his soul, it had to be a powerful one.

CHAPTER 5

Paul had wanted to kiss her so bad, but it was too soon. Way too soon.

The way his magic had touched hers… It had felt almost inevitable. He hadn't felt a magic that complemented his own so well in all his years. Yet, her magic was nascent. Almost completely hidden, with only the slightest bit working its way out here and there.

No wonder someone who could sniff out magic had reported her to the *AC*—or whoever those home invaders had been. She must have been having moments of clarity when her power was leaking out all over the place—probably as she was actively having a vision, as she had in the car, earlier—then it all went under wraps again.

That was why her magic had confused him. It had almost escaped his notice completely, but it was there. And it was powerful. Very powerful.

Maybe even a match for his.

He retrieved the takeout food from the delivery person and locked the door after, adding a little zing of his magic to ward the entry. He'd go through later and put more powerful wards on all the windows, and maybe take a tour around the property and scribe a circle of protection around it. As a witch with unreliable powers, Syd would be most vulnerable until her magic manifested fully and she was able to use it more constructively.

Paul intentionally made a bit of noise setting out the bags of takeout, wanting to put Syd more at ease. He wanted to put her at ease because he had no intention of leaving her alone for what remained of the evening. If he couldn't convince her to let him sleep on her couch, he had every intention of finding a place outside, perhaps in her yard, or maybe even on the roof, from which he could watch over her.

It didn't sit right with him that she'd been reported to the *Venifucus* when she was at such a vulnerable point in her magical development. It would be just like that evil order to seek out magic users as they developed, either to recruit them or eliminate them as possible future threats to their agenda.

Syd appeared a few moments later, and they spent a quiet half hour eating dinner and exchanging the barest minimum of small talk. Paul knew, regardless of the magical treatment he'd been able to administer to her head wound, it still had to hurt. He also knew she had a lot to think about. The poor woman had been through a lot in the past few hours. He let her take her time. He didn't want to push her too hard, but he would finagle a way to stay in her house tonight, if at all possible.

When it finally came down to it, he didn't even have to broach the subject himself. Syd asked him to stay over before they even finished eating.

"You haven't arranged a hotel room yet, right?" she asked out of the blue. He admitted he hadn't with a shake of his head, and she plowed right on. "I know my couch isn't the most comfortable thing in the world, but it's a small house, and I don't have a guest room. You could take my room, I guess—"

"The couch is fine," he cut her off as politely as he could. "Thank you for offering."

As the evening went on, Syd didn't bring up any of the topics Paul expected. He'd thought she'd grill him about magic and shapeshifters and particularly what kind he claimed to be, but instead, she kept the conversation to light topics. His travels, the foods he'd grown up with and the foods he liked here, and those she thought he should try.

She told him about her job at the plant nursery and how she loved working with growing things. She talked about the various kinds of plants that her company specialized in—those native to parts of Mexico, South America, and the American Southwest. She gave him her view on desert landscapes and the unique properties of the mountains around here as compared with the ranges farther north and west.

He was somewhat fascinated by her knowledge of the local flora and conditions in the mountains that he now knew he would have to search carefully. She'd seen dragons in her vision. If, as he suspected, she was a nascent witch with the gift of foresight, just coming into her powers, then he had to give at least some credence to what she'd told him. He'd have to look for his brother dragons there as best he could. For that was his quest. He had traveled the world over, searching for other dragons, and now…finally…it looked as if he was on the right trail.

Or, this all could be some sort of elaborate trap, but he really didn't think so. Gifted with strong magic of his own, Paul had used every trick he knew to test the veracity of what Syd had told him. He'd watched everything from her body language to her magical output to see if she was trying to influence him in some way, but everything he'd seen only convinced him more of her innocence.

He was truly concerned that she was now being hunted. His interference in her affairs had probably drawn more attention to her than if he'd just left the surveillance gear in place, but there really had been no other option. When the leader of that little crew had bopped her on the head, he'd changed the rules completely.

She'd seen them. She knew people had been in her house. In the normal course of events, she probably would've called the cops when she woke up, and they would probably have found at least some of the cameras. Of course, that was if the leader didn't decide to finish what he'd started and just kill her while she was unconscious and save everyone a whole lot of bother.

If those people were really *Venifucus* agents, Paul knew they wouldn't even blink at the idea of killing an innocent. The *Venifucus* had done far more grotesque things in their long history of serving evil. Even if they hadn't killed her, the *Venifucus* had magic of their own—dark, evil stuff that they could use to infect Syd and perhaps turn her growing abilities to their own use.

Yeah, Paul had really had no other choice. He'd had to intervene. So, the question then became, what happened now that the bad guys knew Syd had at least one powerful Other on her side?

Paul shook his head, later that night after Syd had retired to her bedroom on the other side of the cozy house. He was going to sack out on the couch, but not before he spent a little time on her computer, doing some more research. Powered by magic, Paul didn't always require a great deal of sleep, and he was too keyed up from everything he'd learned to nod off now.

He began his research by looking up general information about the mountains and doing his best to learn about the geography of the area. He could cover a lot of distance from the air, but he suspected the real searching would need to be done from the ground. He began by familiarizing himself with the different mountain ranges in the area and then started reading about the legends that had been passed down for centuries about things that were rumored to have happened or been hidden in various places.

Mostly the legends talked about gold. Hidden caverns filled with nearly pure gold ore. In particular, there was one legend that caught his attention—and apparently had sparked human imaginations for the past hundred years and more. That was the tale of the Lost Dutchman Mine.

According to legend, a German immigrant named Jacob Waltz had struck gold in the late 1800s somewhere in the Superstition Mountains. He kept the location of his find secret, leaving only cryptic clues that people still tried to decipher to find the hidden mine. Supposedly, he'd died with a box full of over twenty pounds of very pure gold ore under his bed and had sold a great deal of gold to the United States Mint years before—enough to buy himself a hundred-and-sixty-acre tract of land that he farmed outside of Phoenix.

His farm was all but swept away in the great flood of 1891, and it was believed he contracted pneumonia during the flooding, which later killed him, but not before he'd told someone where to find the mine. That person, the woman who had nursed him during his illness, tried to mount expeditions into the mountains the following year, but no one had ever admitted to finding the mine in all the years since.

Paul sat back, thinking about the story and what he knew of dragons. He'd spent a lot of time doing research in stuffy libraries around the world and on the internet, looking for the merest hint of a legend about his people. Everything he'd read indicated that dragons liked gold and sparkly things. As a dragon himself, Paul had to admit, his eye was drawn by diamonds and precious gems, but he was a practical man at heart. He was more interested in their value as very portable currency than in acquiring them just for the sake of looking at them.

In fact, he never traveled anywhere without a small pouch of gemstones that he kept on his person at all times. When he shifted, the stones went into the shift and came back when he was human again. There were a few gold and silver coins in the pouch as well because gold and silver were much easier to convert into cash these days than precious gems, but gram for gram, the gems were worth more and weighed less, so they were a good way to keep the majority of his assets with him, and safe.

Perhaps that's where the dragon shifters of old had gained their reputation for collecting sparkling objects. Maybe they traveled, as he did, from country to country with ease. Rather than having to worry about carrying around stashes of local currency, Paul had found cashing in a few coins in each new country gave him the operating capital he needed while he was there, and he could turn the cash back into gold easily enough. All it took was a knowledge of the spot price and where to find a coin shop.

Dragons were unique among shifters in being able to travel vast distances in short times. The problem of needing money wherever you landed was easily solved as long as you had a little gold or a few precious stones on you. It made sense to him that the same strategy he had devised would have served other dragon shifters, as well.

Maybe—if Syd's vision was to be believed—a group of dragon shifters were hiding out in an old mine, close to the source of their riches. It would make sense. A ready source of wealth. A hard-to-find cavern. An old mine in the middle of nowhere would make a great hideout for someone who could fly vast distances and navigate rough terrain, who didn't want to be found.

Before Paul put himself down on the couch for a few hours of shut eye, he sent out a few emails to friends and acquaintances he had in Grizzly Cove. First, he was looking for some information on the surveillance gear and had sent some images along with the email, showing the items he had and those that might be going spare. He figured somebody up there would want them.

Second, he needed some contacts on the ground here in Phoenix if at all possible. Paul knew the shifter network was extensive. Even more extensive was the network of ex-military shifters. Most of them were spread out far and wide. It was a rare circumstance that had created Grizzly Cove—a place where almost all the men were former military. Those guys had to have some contacts here that Paul might be able to use. If so, he would need an introduction, and he suspected his newfound cousin up there, the big Kamchatka bear shifter, Peter, would be willing to vouch for him.

Emails sent, Paul shut down the laptop after scrubbing all evidence of what he'd used it for from its drive and cache. He stretched, did a quick tour around the perimeter, placing magical wards as he went, then came back in and sent his magical senses outward, doing a further check before he could settle. He relaxed back on the couch, stretching out his legs and closed his eyes. A few moments later, he was asleep. Alert on one level, but for all intents and purposes, sleeping.

Syd was exhausted after the eventful day. When she'd gone upstairs a few hours after dinner, she'd taken a long, hot shower then fallen into bed almost immediately. She slept hard for the first few hours of the night, but then…the dreams started.

Dreams of being lost, all alone on the dark highway and being attacked by dark wings breathing fire from above. Dreams of reaching out and having her arms burst into flame. Feathery flame that made her rise as she tried to beat them out. Wings. They were wings, she realized after a confused moment. She was a bird made of fire, and she was flying.

At her side was the dark creature in the dark sky. She couldn't see him clearly because the night was pitch black and the lights of the city were far, far away. The terrain below was that of the mountains where Arthur lived. Or near there, somewhere. No man's land, for the most part.

A male dragon flew at her side. She didn't know how she knew the dragon was male, but in the dream, it made sense that he was. He was familiar, somehow.

She let the thought go because—*holy shit*—she was flying! She took a moment to enjoy the sensation, knowing the moment of peace could not last. Somewhere below, evil beckoned. Danger was near, and she would have to face it.

In her darkened bedroom, Syd thrashed on her bed, dislodging sheets and tumbling pillows to the floor. In her dream, fear gripped her. She was spiraling downward, out of control, the dragon beside her. They were fighting for their lives. They would fall to their deaths if something didn't change. But what? What could she do?

And then, she was changing back into her human form, still falling. The dragon beside her changed, too, and he reached out to grab her hand. It was Paul. Syd gasped, falling, falling, falling...

In her bedroom, a hand grasped hers, and she woke with a startled gasp.

Paul was there, holding her hand. Syd sat bolt upright in her disheveled bed, trying to catch her breath. He was sitting on the side of her bed, turned to face her, his gaze held deep concern and that calm inner strength that seemed to be his hallmark.

"What happened? What did you see?" Paul asked, his dark eyes gleaming at her in the dim room.

"You..." she managed, still breathing hard as if she'd run a mile in less than a minute. "You were the..." She wasn't sure she should be saying this, but she had to. She felt compelled to say it. "You were the dragon."

His gaze narrowed, and his lips thinned into a compressed line. He didn't look happy, but she knew what she'd seen. She had no idea what it meant, but she stood by what she had seen.

"Paul. You were the dragon."

His grip on her hand was the only thing keeping her from running away. She held on to him like he was her lifeline, and perhaps, for that moment, he was. He didn't say anything as she tried to get her panic under control. He just held her gaze, his own steadfast and strong. Grounding her...somehow.

"What else did you see?" he asked, after long moments, as her breathing slowed.

"Not much else. I was flying. I was a bird made of fire. A phoenix, I guess, though it makes no sense. And you were flying next to me over the mountains, out near where we met. Where Arthur lives."

"Arthur?" he asked, his head tilting in question.

"An old man. He's actually a retired shaman. I bring him

groceries every once in a while," she explained. "That's what I was doing out there yesterday. That road we were on leads up into the hills, where he lives. Not much else up there. Just a few homesteads, here and there, though not too close together."

"I didn't know a shaman could retire," was Paul's comment, his lips quirking upward in somewhat dry humor.

She didn't know what to say to that observation. She hadn't really ever thought about it before, but that seemed silly now. Arthur had to do *something* with his time. She just had no idea what that something might be.

"You should meet him," she said, a feeling of rightness accompanying the words she hadn't even known she was going to speak until they came out of her mouth. As she thought about it, though, it made a lot of sense. "He's the only person I've told about my visions aside from you."

"When did you tell him?" Paul asked, his tone still concerned, but gentle.

"Earlier today. That's why I stayed so long at his place. I had to work up the courage to ask him about it, and that took some time. I didn't really broach the subject until shortly before I would have normally left. I don't like to get caught up there after dark, so I usually leave him at least an hour before sunset, so I'll have enough time to get back to the highway before night falls."

"It couldn't have been him, then," Paul said, looking to the side briefly, as if deep in thought. "I assume you were together the whole time? He couldn't have made any phone calls or sent any texts while you were with him, right?"

"Yes. His house is small. I'd have heard or seen anything like that," she admitted.

"Then, in all likelihood, it's just your co-worker's actions that set the dogs on your trail," he told her, speaking quietly, with a slight edge to his voice.

She didn't like thinking about the weasel who had ratted her out. Her hand tightened unconsciously on Paul's, which made her realize they were still holding hands, their fingers entwined. When she tried to move away, he resisted, tugging her closer, instead.

Her gaze met his...and held. Suddenly, the atmosphere in the dark room changed. Became more intimate. She wanted, more than anything, to feel his lips on hers. To learn the texture and shape of them. The taste of him.

They were alone in her darkened bedroom in the middle of the night. There was no one here to judge them. No prying eyes—thanks to his work in removing the cameras that had been installed all over her home—to see what they got up to. Nobody to frown at her neediness.

It had been a hell of a day. Surely, taking a bit of comfort from another being wasn't asking too much. She'd felt so alone out there on the highway—and again, when she'd walked in to find the sanctity of her home totally violated. Both times, Paul had come to her...helped her...made her feel not so alone. Not so completely isolated. As if she had someone in her life, however temporarily, who actually cared.

Was it too bad of her to want to take that one step further? If she was reading him right, he wanted it, too. Something that felt so right, surely, couldn't be wrong. She leaned closer to him, her eyes drifting closed as she breathed in the scent of him. Spice and cinnamon, with a hint of...smoke? Not tobacco smoke. Something earthier. Like charcoal.

And then, all thought fled as his lips touched hers for the first time.

Without conscious thought, she let her hands rise up to encircle his neck, feeling the full sensual impact of his kiss. She didn't fight. She didn't reject. Rather, she reveled in the way his lips took hers, his kiss full of the mastery he had displayed in every other action she had seen him perform.

Would he be as masterful in bed? When he was inside her?

It was too soon to let him into her bed, but something about the way he touched her made it feel inevitable. What was she waiting for? It was clear she wanted him, and judging by the way his tongue dueled with hers—so perfectly—he wanted her, too.

She didn't resist when he pushed gently on her shoulders, laying her back down on her bed, her head hitting the pillow. He came down over her, his mouth still joined to hers, the fingers of one hand splayed in her hair, holding her head gently in place as he took the kiss to a new level. His other hand moved downward, caressing, pausing here and there, touching and learning her shape.

She lifted herself against him, wanting more contact. Her body ached for his possession, and she gave up pretending she wasn't going to do this. If he wanted to go all the way, she was not going to deny him. She'd been through so much since meeting him, she needed this.

There was something about him that touched her on a primal level and had since the moment she first encountered him on that dark and dusty road. She ran her fingers into the hair at the nape of his neck, loving the feel of him, the heat of his skin against her hands. He ran hot—in more ways than one.

Wherever he touched her, she felt on fire. She wouldn't be surprised if they were leaving little scorch marks all over her sheets, they were so combustible together. But she didn't mind. Not in the least. No, she wanted more of his fire. More of his scalding, tempting touch.

When he gave it to her, his hand cupping her breast, she moaned into his mouth. Yes. That's what she wanted. That, and more. Oh, so much more.

He squeezed her soft flesh, reminding her that her breasts were erogenous zones. The men she'd been with in the past hadn't known much about foreplay if these few moments with Paul were any indication. He didn't rush anything. He spent time learning her, kissing and touching, stroking and *feeling*. She'd never been so thoroughly kissed in her life.

When he finally lifted his head away from hers, his lips lingering until the last possible moment, their eyes met...and held. She saw fire reflected in his eyes, but it didn't frighten her. In that moment, they were creatures of flame. Creatures of desire. Both wanting to touch the inferno that was brewing within their souls.

"Are you all right with this?" Paul asked, his voice deep and growly in a way that made her tummy clench. *Sexy.*

She nodded, not sure what words to use that wouldn't make her sound like a harlot. Paul, it seemed, didn't want to let her off that easy.

"I want to hear you say it, *draga.*"

His whispered words lit fires in her soul. Good fires. Warming fires. Fires she never wanted extinguished. She didn't know what the word *draga* meant, but it sounded good. Fierce and sweet, the way he said it. Like he cared.

"Make me forget everything but you, Paul," she said, honesty baring her soul.

She couldn't claim to love him. Not after such a short acquaintance, but that's sort of what it felt like. Maybe she was letting her imagination run away with her. Maybe she was delusional. And maybe, it didn't matter. Not right now, anyway.

One thing was clear, after the events of the past day. She knew, without doubt, she could count on him when the going got tough. He'd been there for her in ways nobody had ever been before. He'd stood up for her. He'd challenged some pretty tough guys on her behalf. He'd protected her when she was injured and couldn't take care of herself. Everything he had done since they first met had displayed the heart of gold in his chest, and that deep well of honor that sprang from his soul.

He was a good man. Of that, she had no doubt. Her instincts confirmed the evidence of the past hours. And the attraction she had felt almost from the first could no longer be denied.

It might be self-indulgent. It might even be a little slutty. But she knew, in her heart, that if she made love with Paul right now, she wouldn't have any regrets in the morning. The only thing she would regret forever was if she turned him away now.

"Is that all?" he pushed, wanting more. "You just want to forget?"

She shook her head, trying to find the words and not sure how he would handle the truth. She felt so much for him, so fast. Most guys didn't want to hear that kind of thing on such short acquaintance. She bit her lip in indecision, but he tapped her upper lip with one finger, coaxing her to release the lower one.

"I want more than that," she told him, deciding to be daring. "I want you, Paul."

His sexy smile lit her world. "Then, you shall have me." He dipped his head closer to lick at her lips, biting gently on the lower one then releasing it. She found the move almost unbearably exciting. "And...I shall have you," he finished, naughty promises in his eyes that she couldn't wait to be fulfilled.

CHAPTER 6

Syd gasped as Paul lowered more of his weight onto her. He was so solid. So warm and masculine. So much more than any man she'd ever had before. She had a momentary thought that, after this, she might well be ruined for all others. If that was to be her fate, she decided to embrace it fully. Embrace *him* fully. For this night might never come again. While she had him here, she was going to savor the experience and do her best not to think of the future at all.

That thought firmly in mind, she began to touch him in daring ways. Ways she hadn't tried with the other men she'd been with. She reached for Paul, stroking her hands over every inch she could reach, letting her impatient fingers work on the buttons of his shirt, the zip of his jeans. She wanted him naked, and she wanted it now.

But he had other ideas. Paul slowed her, impeding her progress with gentle movements. Focusing his attention on her body. Her pleasure. Her enticement.

It was something none of her former lovers had ever done. Of course, there hadn't been that many, but she had some experience. Paul was making her feel like an utter novice once again. He didn't think only of his own pleasure, rushing her to the finish line. Rather, he seemed to not even be aware there was a finish line, so to speak. He made her aware of the here. The now. The infinitesimal moment when his touch lit her world with incandescent pleasure…and the promise of oh, so much more.

Wow. Her head was spinning already, and they were both still mostly dressed. He'd loosened her top, but it was still mostly on. She wanted it gone. She wanted his shirt gone, too, so she could feel the texture and heat of his skin against hers. She wanted to feel him body to body, all over. As soon as possible.

Again, Paul appeared to have other ideas. He undressed her with unhurried calm and heated touches that sent her senses into orbit. Forget flying, she was going intergalactic. His touch, and his talented lips and tongue, sent her higher than she'd ever been before without actually climaxing. She wasn't sure, based on what she was feeling right now, if she would survive an orgasm with Paul, but she was desperate to find out.

When he finally divested her of her shirt and bra, she waited for him to pounce. Instead, he leaned back to just look at her. She could feel her nipples tightening as his gaze wrapped her in approval and desire. She'd never had a man look at her like that. Not once, in all her life.

Yes, sir. She'd been right. Being with Paul could become addictive, but at the moment, she didn't mind. She'd happily become an addict if he'd just keep looking at her like that…and more.

"*Vrei sa fii tu steaua mea norocoasa?*" he whispered in what had to be Romanian, his mother tongue.

"What does that mean?" she whispered back. Paul shook his head slightly and smiled.

"Sorry. I asked if you wanted to be my lucky star." He looked a little sheepish. "It sounds better in Romanian."

"It's charming," she told him, reaching up to stroke her fingers through his dark hair. He was so incredibly handsome in a rugged, strong way. She was quickly becoming fascinated with every little detail about him. "And the answer is yes, in case you were in any doubt," she told him in a quiet voice, a shy grin on her lips before he lowered his head and claimed her mouth again in a kiss hotter than any other he'd given her to this point.

Things began to move a lot faster after that. Where before, he'd seemed to want to savor, now, he seemed driven by need. Her clothing disappeared under his skilled hands, as did his. She had the vague idea that he just threw all the clothes toward the corner of her bedroom, but she wasn't sure. Wherever they'd gone, she was glad they could no longer interfere with the sensations she'd longed to feel.

Skin on skin. Desire and heat. Need and acceptance. It was all there. Everything she'd ever dreamed of but had never found with a lover.

It was perfect. And, in that perfect moment, he slid into her for the first time, making her gasp. It was a simple joining. Man on top in the traditional way, but that didn't mean it was boring or routine. Not in the least.

Paul began to move almost at once, as if he was losing control over the game of desire he'd played until this point. It was the sexiest thing he'd done to date. The idea that she could make him lose it fired her confidence in her own femininity and made her want, more than anything, to be an equal partner in this seduction of the senses.

She met him move for move, thrust for thrust, participating fully in the act that she began to realize would alter her fate in some way. Like all her premonitions, she didn't know how she knew what she knew, but she did. Something big was happening here.

And she wasn't just thinking about the part of him that was buried deep inside her at the moment. That thought made her smile at her own silliness a moment before Paul changed up the pace, doing something that made his cock hit a spectacular place inside her she hadn't known existed. She screamed his name as she came, and he kept going, making her climax last and last.

It was like nothing she'd ever experienced before as pleasure sent her body into spasms of intensity. Multiple times. *Holy cow!* Multiple orgasms. She'd thought that was just a myth, but Paul was proving the incredible reality to her. Over and over again.

When he finally joined her in ecstasy, after wringing every last bit of pleasure out of her body that he possibly could, she was more than ready to return the favor. Her body clamped around him as he went rigid in her arms. She watched his face, his eyes closed as pleasure washed over him. He was an amazing man who had already given her more than any other man she'd ever known, both in pleasure and in safety.

He'd helped her. He'd probably saved her life twice over. And now, he'd introduced her to a new level of lovemaking she hadn't known existed.

What an incredible man.

Paul couldn't believe the pleasure to be found in Syd's arms. The experience of being with her made all other sexual experiences he'd ever had pale into insignificance. He wasn't sure what it was about her—or what had just happened here—but he knew he had to stick around to at least try to figure it out. There was something very special about Syd, and he wanted to learn all her secrets before they went their separate ways. That was...if he could bear to leave her after this.

At this point, he wasn't at all sure he'd be able to make himself go.

As they began to come down from the most intense sexual peak of his life, Paul couldn't speak. He just tucked her into his arms, making them comfortable on her big bed, then let the moment fade into sleep. He'd have time to think about everything in the morning. For now, they both needed to recharge and rest.

Paul woke briefly a few hours later, when an attempt was made to breach the ward he'd put up near the side of the house. Someone or something had tried to enter through one of the ground-floor windows, but the ward—coupled with some of the surveillance gear he'd re-used for his own purposes—had scared them off. Nothing like using their own motion sensors, hooked to a lamp in the room, against them.

They'd no doubt triggered the motion sensor he'd aimed at the window, and the lamp had lit, making them think someone was about to discover their attempted intrusion. The magical ward he'd put around every opening into the house had told him instantly which window had been tried, and he also knew that no one had successfully entered the house.

Syd slept on, serene in his arms, and he decided the intruders could wait until the morning. He wasn't about to get out of this cozy bed with the woman who was fast becoming important to him to look at a cold trail. For, he had no doubt, the intruders would not try that window again.

They probably wouldn't try anything else that night, but if they did, he would know the instant it happened. If someone managed to get in, he wouldn't mind going dragon on their ass if they threatened his woman.

That's when he realized he was thinking of Syd not just as *a* woman, but as *his* woman. Hmm. That was somewhat startling to realize, but he couldn't work up any real energy to question it further at that moment. Not when sleep was calling his name, and he had a warm, sensual, giving woman in his arms. He let it go for now. He'd think about everything later. This moment was for savoring.

Paul woke again a couple of hours later. Another attempt had been made on one of the windows, and the intruder had been rebuffed again. He had to give them points for persistence, but so far, they hadn't demonstrated that they had enough firepower, magically speaking, to overcome his wards. They also didn't seem to realize he'd rigged their own surveillance gear against them. They probably hadn't thought anyone could do so that fast, but Paul was good with electronics and had realized years ago that he had something of a talent for it.

Still, the continued attempts to get in made him realize

that Syd was very vulnerable. If he wasn't here, she wouldn't know about any attempted intrusions, much less that there was probably a team waiting outside her door to abduct her—or worse—given half the chance. What if she went outside to water the garden, or put out the trash, or any one of a hundred possible things that could make her leave the protection of her newly-warded home?

She didn't have the skills to deal with physical threats—or magical ones—and Paul couldn't spend every moment with her from now on. No. He would need backup if he wanted to keep her safe, and that meant making contact with some locals he could trust. With any luck, his friends in Grizzly Cove would have seen his messages and replied by morning, and he could work on getting some real security help to safeguard Syd. Hopefully, by later today, if all went well.

Paul silently marveled at how easily he'd adapted to having found relatives—albeit distant relatives—in Grizzly Cove. For a loner who'd been orphaned as a baby and had never known what it was to have family, Paul had not only been accepted with open arms by the bear shifters he'd found that likely shared an ancestor with him, but he'd come to depend on them in ways he'd never depended on anyone before.

It was nice, having a family. It was something he'd always wanted and had now found, to a greater degree than he'd expected, but his quest continued. Finding other dragons was his goal, and if Syd could help him do it, then he would stick to her like glue and keep her safe against her enemies. No matter what.

Of course, after last night, his reasons for wanting to keep her safe and staying with her had become ever more complex. There was indescribable pleasure involved now, as well as genuine feelings. It was all a little confusing, but at the heart of it, it was really very simple. He liked her. He cared for her. He wanted to make love with her as often as she'd let him, and he didn't want that to stop…ever.

Wow. Talk about things moving fast.

Then, there was the possibility that she could lead him to

more dragon shifters. It was what had drawn him to her from the beginning, but now, the relationship had evolved—in only a few short hours—into something that had him thinking about the future and how to keep her with him for years to come.

That's the moment he was thinking in terms of years. Decades, even. Everything he had been able to discover about dragon shifters indicated that they lived an extraordinarily long life. Bear shifters were among the most magical of common shifter species, and they routinely lived at least three centuries, if they didn't die due to warfare or other injury. Dragon shifters were a lot more magical, which meant a much longer life.

Which begged the question—was Syd the kind of woman that could be a true mate, or was she a temporary partner in life? Was she a human magic user with a human lifespan who would share a few decades with him, then break his heart by dying? Or was she something else? Could she be the true mate that could share in his magic...and his years?

There were legends about that kind of thing, but Paul was still woefully unknowledgeable about his own kind. This was the kind of question he could've asked his parents—if he had ever known them. As it was, he was unprepared and not sure what to think about any of this.

Regardless, they had more immediate problems. Another of his wards rang with an attempted intrusion. Enough was enough.

Easing out from Syd's bed so as not to wake her, he decided it was time to singe a few tails. Hopefully, that would allow him to rest a little longer with the woman who was quickly coming to mean everything to him.

Paul went through the house, room by room, window by window, and reinforced his wards with something that would offer a bit more zip the next time some jackass tried to breach his magical protections. A yelp sounded, not ten minutes later, as he was finishing up. He went over to the room on the first floor that Syd used as an office and stood quietly in the window, where anyone outside could see him.

Casually, he looked down to find one of the team members from earlier in the evening, lying prone on the grass a few feet from the window. He'd been shocked and thrown, his body still twitching, though he was conscious. He took one look at Paul standing in the window and started a rapid, awkward crab walk backwards, away from the house. As soon as he was able to stand—the effect of the zap wearing off a bit—he did so and turned tail to run into the trees at the edge of the property.

Paul watched him go, smiling. He let his teeth lengthen just the tiniest bit in a micro-shift. Let them wonder what he was. Shifter or even bloodletter. Keep them guessing. Let them realize they were up against something they hadn't counted on. That ought to get them to leave Syd alone for a while.

Paul knew he was just buying time. Hopefully, they'd leave Syd be long enough for Paul to get backup in place. He just needed a few hours. Half a day, at most. Judging by the response so far from the team that had infiltrated Syd's house earlier, they didn't have the kind of firepower they'd need to be a serious threat—but he'd bet they could get it.

The race was on to see whose backup would arrive first.

That thought in mind, Paul left the window with one last disgusted glance and went into the main living area, picking a spot where he wouldn't be readily visible from outside. He'd closed all the curtains and blinds he could, but there were a few windows that didn't have either. He'd fix that later today, if Syd was willing.

And he'd spend what was left of the night convincing her to be *willing*, if necessary. He looked forward to it. But, first, he accessed his cell phone and checked messages.

Bingo. Cousin Peter had come through. He had a contact name and location for Paul to try in the morning. He'd even promised to call ahead and tell his contact that Paul was on his way. In the shifter community—particularly among ex-military shifters—it really helped to have someone on the inside of that community vouch for you. With Peter's introduction, things should go a lot smoother with the local shifters, and Paul hoped he would find some willing to help Syd out.

According to what Peter had to say about his friends in this town, they sounded like just the sort of people Paul needed. Ex-military with honed skills in protecting high-value targets. Value couldn't get much higher than Syd's life and freedom. Paul would be sure to impress that upon any shifter who agreed to help.

Before that, though, he still had a few hours in the night left to be with her. He went back to her bedroom and climbed back in her bed. She rolled over and snuggled into him, waking a little.

"Where did you go?" she asked, her voice low and scratchy with sleep. Sexy.

"Just checking things," he told her. He would not worry her right now with the knowledge that there had been multiple attempts to get into the house in just the past few hours.

She seemed to wake up a little more, leaning up on one elbow to look at his face. He didn't like the little worry line between her eyebrows, so he decided to distract her. He slid his hands down to her hips and coaxed her over to straddle his body. He was naked once more, though he'd put on his jeans to prowl around the house earlier, and his cock was ready for action, as it seemed to be whenever he got within touching distance of Syd. Damn. The woman could lead him around by the balls if she ever realized her power over him, but he already knew she wasn't that kind of woman. No, any power she had, she would use for good. Or, so he believed.

Maybe he was being naïve. Maybe he was too trusting. Or, maybe, he'd found a genuine pearl on a dark mountain road.

As she discovered his readiness, the worry line between her delicate brows lifted, and interest kindled in her eyes, as he'd hoped. She surprised him, becoming the aggressor, reaching down to align their bodies before sliding onto him, holding his gaze throughout. He gasped.

"Damn, woman," he ground out, his passion going from zero to a hundred and sixty in nothing flat.

"What? You don't like it?" she teased, pretending to lift away, but his hands on her hips stopped her and brought her back down on his hard cock as she made a humming sound of pure pleasure.

"You know damned well that I do," he told her, reaching up to cup her breasts in his palms. She was so beautifully made. Everything about her was luscious and perfect. What he considered perfect, anyway. Perfect for him.

Syd didn't know what made her so bold, only that she liked being on top, and she liked the fire in his eyes as Paul looked at her. The heat of his touch sparked an answering fire in her own body as she began to move on him, taking him deeper with each new stroke.

There was something about Paul that made her do things she hadn't dared before. He made her want things. Want *him*. In ways she didn't yet fully understand. Long-term ways. *Permanent* ways.

But, no. She couldn't think about the future—especially not a future with Paul. She couldn't count on anything where he was concerned. In fact, she couldn't count on anything where her own life was concerned just now. It all had gotten so strange lately. So confusing.

This, however... This was an electrifying connection...between herself and Paul on the most basic level. This was delicious. Captivating. Addictive.

She decided, then and there, to enjoy every moment. Every stroke. Every climax. And, judging by their previous encounter, there would be many of those. Just the idea of it made her shiver as she picked up her pace.

In charge this time, she wanted to make it as good for him as he'd made it for her earlier. She tried different things. She altered her pace. Shifted her position slightly. Watched his face for any hint that what she tried worked for him.

In those moments of trying to please him, she learned things about him...but also about her own pleasure. The intensity rose higher and higher until she almost couldn't stand it, anymore. She knew she was about to lose control completely, but she knew he'd be there to catch her. She already trusted him to take care of her when the crisis hit, and she wasn't disappointed.

She cried out as she came, her body trembling around him. Then, he did as she'd known he would. He clamped his hands down on her hips, sliding deep before coaxing her to lay down over him. Then, he rolled, taking them both to their sides, where he positioned them as he wished while her ardor cooled only slightly.

Paul tugged her upper leg over his hip and began a new rhythm as he thrust into her. The angle was different. Interesting and...oh, yeah...delicious. Another orgasm hit before she knew what was happening, and then another.

She held on for the ride as he brought her to pleasure after pleasure before finally joining her in climax. She might've blacked out for a moment, but she wasn't quite sure. Her mind just shut down for a few seconds as rapture shot through her like a flame tornado. The only solid thing in the midst of it all was Paul. His hands, his hard body, his ultra-masculine presence next to her, around her...inside her.

He was her only anchor to the real world, and she knew in her deepest heart that he would keep her safe. How she knew it, she had no idea, but the thought rang with truth as it rolled around her sluggish mind. Coming back to the world was a long, delectable process, broken only by Paul's care of her body while her spirit was still flying.

He tucked her in, next to his warm body, covering her with the sheet and putting the cover nearby if she wanted it. He was both thoughtful and considerate. Yummy.

That was the last coherent thought she had before she fell asleep again, next to the man who had become more important to her in the past few hours than any man had in years. She should have been stunned by the rapid progress of their fledgling relationship, but she was too wrung out from the best sex of her life to really think about it.

CHAPTER 7

Paul was making breakfast when Syd padded downstairs in sock feet. Nevertheless, he heard her every move. His hearing was that good. Plus, he seemed to be more attuned to her now, after their night together. It was strange, but ever since he'd woken up at dawn with her in his arms, he'd felt it. A closeness he'd never felt before with any other woman.

He'd thought he'd surprise her with breakfast in bed, but she'd awoken shortly after he started cooking. She'd showered and dressed while he put together a big meal out of the supplies in her fridge. Eggs, bacon, and toast with butter and jam. He'd thought about making pancakes, as well, but she was human—or mostly human, with a touch of foresight—and she probably wouldn't eat as much as a shifter woman.

When she appeared in the archway, she was wearing jean shorts and a shirt bearing the logo of a local nursery. The nursery where she worked, he surmised. It looked like she was intending on going into work today.

That made him pause. He'd been thinking she'd stay home, and he had been planning to impress upon her the need to stay inside while he arranged for backup, but this changed things. He started recalculating his plans. If she wanted to go to work, he wasn't really in any position to demand she stay home—much as he wished he could. She had a life of her own that didn't include him…yet. She had responsibilities and commitments, and he had to find a way to respect that while still making sure she was safe until he'd earned the right to be a more complete part of her life.

He was realizing, more and more, that's exactly what he wanted. He felt a pull to become her partner, her mate. He didn't fully understand it all, but he wasn't really questioning things too closely right now. So much was happening. So much change. This was just one more in a series of upheavals that had brought him here, to this place, at this time…with this woman, who might very well hold the key to his future, both as a dragon and as a man.

"I take it you have to work today," he asked, trying his best not to sound confrontational. Women didn't like being given ultimatums. He'd learned that back in Romania, with his first girlfriend, a spitfire named Katya, who had left him after his dominant traits started to shine through a bit too much.

"I know it'd be safer not to go in, but I have to pay the bills, and frankly, I want to see if Elliot is there, and if so, what he does when he sees me." She had a light of combat in her eye that impressed Paul, even as it made him wary.

"Are you planning to confront him?" Paul didn't like the sound of that at all.

"I don't know what I plan to do. I have no plan. I'm just winging it, but if that little toad so much as makes a funny face at me, I'll probably want to punch him in the nose."

Paul motioned for her to sit and placed breakfast in front of her. "You have time for breakfast, right?" he asked, pretty sure she did, but wanting to be sure.

"Yes, thank you. You really didn't have to go to all this trouble, but I appreciate it. I don't think any man has ever made such an effort for me." She sounded truly touched, which also touched his surprisingly gentle heart. He could easily get used to pampering this woman.

"It's my pleasure," he told her, taking his seat by her side before they began to eat. After they'd each eaten a few bites, he restarted the conversation. "So, you work at the greenhouse?"

"I'm sort of a plant doctor. I oversee the greenhouse operation for Stanley, the owner of the nursery. Elliot—the toad—works in the office. He's some kind of bean counter."

"Does that mean you normally don't cross paths often with him?" Paul was trying to get a feel for the setup of her workplace.

"Not too often, though, I guess, now that I think about it, his desk is by a window that looks out into the greenhouse where I do most of my work. The little bastard has probably been watching me from his office." She sounded angry to Paul, which he supposed, on reflection, was better than being scared. Anger could give her strength while fear could cripple.

"Is there a way you could stay out of sight of that window today? Is it possible?" Paul asked.

Syd appeared to think about it as she ate more of the eggs he'd prepared for her. "I think so," she finally answered. "I have some tasks that can be done out front, in the public spaces of the nursery."

"Public is probably better for now. I don't think Elliot, or the people he's in contact with, will be able to make a move on you at work, but there is the possibility, and I want you to be aware of it. I cannot watch over you for a few hours this morning. I must seek allies here in town, in case this problem grows beyond what I alone can handle," he told her. He'd decided he would be as honest as possible with her.

"You have friends here?" She seemed almost hurt by the idea, and he realized she thought he had been lying to her when he'd claimed no familiarity with the area.

"Not friends," he clarified. "But there is a network of sorts that I can call on. I made contact with my relatives in the Pacific Northwest overnight, and my cousin, Peter, sent me a name and address. I must go there this morning to meet the people who might be able to help. If it works out as I hope, you will soon have Others watching over your house so that it cannot be violated as it was last night."

"Others?" she asked sharply, looking up at him with an intensity in her gaze. "Shapeshifters?" she whispered, as if speaking a great secret.

Paul couldn't help but smile softly at her obvious awe at the idea. "Yes. My cousin in a bear shifter. Although he didn't specify the animal spirit of the man he is sending me to meet, I suspect either another werebear or something very similar. Either way, if he is vouched for by Peter, then he is a good man who will not betray us to our enemies."

"How can you be so sure?" she asked, wariness in her gaze now.

"It is hard to explain to someone who has grown up entirely in the human world, but magical folk are pretty evenly split down the middle. Either we serve the Light or the dark. I chose the Light many years ago, though I will admit, due to the nature of my upbringing, I thought, for a while, things would turn out the other way. As an adult, however, I have come to an understanding with the Lady and Her Light. I serve the cause of good and fight evil wherever I find it, as it tries to destroy me and all those who serve the Light."

"You're able to recognize your enemies so easily?"

"Not always, but usually, they can't help but give themselves away at some point, and then, it's game on, as you Americans say." His grin was gentle, but he knew there was probably a lethal edge to it that he wasn't able to hide.

Then again, he had decided not to hide his true nature from this woman. At least...he would share with her what he could, when he could. He would not reveal all in one go. That would probably send her running away from him, into the night. No, he would go slow—or, as slowly as he could manage—in telling her and showing her all that he was and all that he wanted from life...and from her.

They both returned their attention to their meals, finishing the food in silence. When they were done, Paul took the plates, rinsed them, and placed them in the dishwasher for her while Syd gathered her things. Keys in hand, she turned to him.

"How are you planning to get around?" A little frown line appeared between her brows.

He didn't have an answer for her. Frankly, he hadn't thought that far ahead yet. He'd get to the address either by public transportation or, perhaps, he could hire a car to take him. He was about to share his thoughts with her when she tossed him her keys.

"You do have a driver's license, don't you?" He nodded. "Good. You can drop me off at work, then go do your errands. Just don't forget to pick me up at four, okay?"

"I will return your car to the nursery's parking lot as soon as I am finished," he told her. "I'll be there when you get off work, and we can come back here together."

He would be there all day—from the time he returned the car until she was ready to leave—watching over her, but he wouldn't tell her that. For one thing, he would blend in using some of his very potent magic. He had a little investigating he wanted to do, as well. Paul had every intention of observing this Elliot creature as closely as he could. He wanted to know the enemy and whether Elliot was a real threat or merely a nuisance.

Plan made, they walked out to the car together. Paul wouldn't let her get in until he'd had a walk around to physically check that the car had not been tampered with overnight. He had placed wards, as well, and checked them to make sure they had not been crossed. When he saw that all was well, he unlocked the doors, and they got in, heading for her workplace.

*

Paul pulled into the drive of the address he'd been given to find himself in a very high-end car repair lot. Syd's old beater was completely outclassed by the Italian sportscar parked next to it, but Paul didn't mind. He was more interested in the contact he would make here, and his eyes scanned the lot continuously, pegging more than one shifter working in the big yard filled with very expensive automobiles. Interesting.

Paul slid his sunglasses into the front of his T-shirt by one earpiece as he walked into the lobby, meeting the gaze of a sharp-eyed gal who had to be some kind of cat shifter, if he didn't miss his guess. Not a lion or tiger, but something local to North America. Something cuter, if her size was anything to go by.

"May I help you?" She glanced up from her computer screen as he walked in, and her eyes grew round in alarm as she took him in. Hmm. So, the little cat sensed the predator in him. He wasn't sure whether that would help or hinder his search.

"I'm looking for King Bishop. I've been told he works here." Paul tried to sound bored and not at all predatory.

"I'm sorry, King is not here today," she answered promptly, looking a little less frightened but still incredibly curious, which was what led him to believe she was feline.

"Are either of his brothers here, then? Ace or Jack? My cousin in Grizzly Cove sent me here especially to contact them," he revealed, hoping the little cat girl would know what that meant.

Some more of her fear leached away, and he knew the message had been received. He had friends in the Cove, and she knew what that meant. Bear shifters. She likely thought his immense presence was that of another bear, which probably helped calm her nerves. Fine with him. There was no reason to reveal exactly what he was. Not at this point.

"I'm really sorry. All three of them are on leave. As far as I know, they're not even in the state. Maybe Lance can tell you more." She looked apologetic now.

"Lance?" he queried. Peter had only given him the three bear brothers' names. Nobody else.

"The owner of this establishment. Oh," she looked out the glass door behind him, "here he comes now."

Paul turned to see two men approaching. One reached for

77

the door handle, allowing the other to precede him. Paul felt the impact of the first man to enter as a blaze of fire against his personal wards. Not offensive magic. It was just the presence of the man...and it was something Paul didn't recognize, but it felt somehow familiar. There was no doubt in Paul's mind that this fellow was something new, and intensely powerful, but he didn't know exactly what.

The newcomer stopped short as he realized Paul was in the room. The other man entered and moved to the first man's side, a slight snarl emanating from his throat. That sounded distinctly wolf-like to Paul's trained ears. A strong wolf. Perhaps the local Alpha. His actions, though, had already shown he deferred to the first man. So, whatever that first guy was, he was higher in the shifter pecking order than a werewolf Alpha. Things were beginning to get interesting.

"This man was looking for King," the helpful receptionist put him from behind Paul. He'd turned his back on her, assessing her as of little threat compared to the men now facing him—especially that one guy with the fiery presence. "He said he had a cousin in Grizzly Cove who sent him here."

The first guy nodded at the girl and focused on Paul. "I'm Lance. I own the place."

"Paul Lebchenko." He didn't offer his hand. That was too risky among magic folk and not something done lightly. "My cousin, Peter Zilakov, sent me here looking for some friends of his."

"Why?" Lance asked simply, his head tilting to one side as if he was evaluating Paul's words.

Paul had to make a decision—whether to trust his instincts, which told him that these people, no matter how powerful, were not evil, or to just excuse himself and go elsewhere looking for backup. He went with Plan A, hoping he was doing the right thing. In all his experience, he'd never come across a being with as much magic as his own, but he suspected this Lance fellow came close, if indeed, he didn't surpass Paul. If they had to fight, it would be a close match.

"I need help," Paul replied, taking his chances.

Lance frowned. "What kind of help could we give a…well…someone like you?"

Paul was surprised by the way Lance stumbled over his words. Did he think Paul was a bear shifter? Or was he referring to the idea that Paul might be an ex-military shifter like so many of the guys who now lived in Grizzly Cove? Either way, Lance looked uncomfortable, which was odd, since it was obvious to Paul he had immense power of his own.

"A woman I know here in Phoenix has been targeted by the *Venifucus,* though they claim to be *Altor Custodis.* They invaded her house and attempted to put monitoring devices all over it. She walked in on them, and they assaulted her." He told them the bare bones of the story.

"Is she all right?" Lance asked at the same time as his companion growled deeper in his throat.

"I stopped them, and she's okay for now, but I need some help with backup in case they return. They tried multiple times last night to break through my wards, so I suspect they definitely will try for her again. She's a complete innocent. She has a bit of a gift but did not grow up in our world. She knows very little and is at a delicate stage of her development, which is probably why they are targeting her. I suspect they will continue to either try to turn her to their cause, or eliminate her completely."

Lance's frown deepened, but he didn't say anything right away. Instead, he turned to his companion and made introductions.

"This is Stone," Lance said absently. Stone stopped growling long enough to nod at Paul. Lance spoke to Stone next. "What do you think?"

Stone looked Paul up and down before replying. "I don't think he's a bear."

CHAPTER 8

Paul would have laughed had the situation not been so tense. As it was, he couldn't control the little smile he knew broke over his lips. Perhaps it was that which broke the tension in the air, but Stone and Lance both seemed to back down their intensity a hair, which helped Paul do the same.

"My cousin, Peter, is a Kamchatka bear. One of the biggest in the world," Paul told them, shaking his head. "But you're right. I do not share his animal spirit."

"What are you, then?" Lance asked, breaking one of the taboos shifters grew up with. It was considered very rude to just ask. If you couldn't figure it out, then you had to find out in other ways, but asking direct wasn't done.

That told Paul a bit more about Lance. His hesitancy to speak of Paul's other half and his apparent confusion all led Paul to believe that Lance was new to his powers. Whatever they might be. Whatever it was, Lance was something incredibly strong, and fire was his element. Perhaps he was a magic user. A fire-witch of some kind?

No. Paul sensed a duality of spirit that indicated Lance was a type of shifter, but whatever it was that shared his soul, it was something Paul had never encountered before. Stone cringed but quickly erased the expression from his face. The wolf Alpha was loyal to Lance, that much was clear.

Paul was saved from answering by the opening of the door behind Lance and Stone. The moment Paul saw the man who had entered, his face broke into a big grin. He was definitely among the good guys if Slade was friends with these two clowns.

Slade stopped short in the doorway, catching sight of Paul as their eyes met.

"Lebchenko?" Slade said, clearly surprised, though he was also smiling. "What the hell are you doing here?"

"Slade, my old friend. It is good to see you again. I did not know you had moved to these parts," Paul said, truly glad to see the mysterious cat shifter he had befriended long ago in a place far from here.

"You know this guy?" Stone asked as Slade made to move past him to get to Paul. Slade paused and turned to look at Lance and Stone.

"I have known Paul for years. He's on the right side. Or, at least…" Slade turned to give Paul a hard look. "He was the last time I saw him." Slade grinned and closed the distance, reaching out with one hand for a strong handshake accompanied by a back-thumping bro hug. "I can see not much has changed. Still searching?"

"Always," Paul replied. Slade was one of the few people Paul had trusted with knowledge of his past and his ongoing search for others of his kind. "But I believe I'm getting closer."

"Glad to hear it," Slade said, moving back to regard Paul with a friendly smile and easy stance. The others seemed intrigued as the tension in the room ratcheted down another few notches. "What do you need?"

"Backup," Paul answered succinctly. "There is a woman in danger, and I cannot do all the guarding myself. Especially when I do not know the full extent of the threat yet."

Paul took a few moments to fill in Slade on the situation with Syd and those who had invaded her house. At Slade's questioning, Paul gave them all more details about what had happened, and what he suspected. This time, when he went through the facts, he got more the reaction he'd been looking for from the beginning. Slade's brows drew together in concern, and his lips thinned into a grim line.

It was Lance who noticed that customers were heading for the lobby. He nodded toward the window and suggested they move to his office, and all four of them did so in short order. The office was big enough to hold them all without being overcrowded, though there was a great deal of magic present between the wolf Alpha, Slade, Paul, and whatever Lance was.

They spent about a half hour discussing options for surveillance coverage, which was where Stone proved his worth. It would be his Pack members doing the legwork on this one, and Paul was grateful to find the werewolf was willing to help once Slade had vouched for Paul's character. The impromptu meeting broke up as Stone headed out to talk to his people. He promised to have someone at the nursery within the hour to keep an eye on things. Paul thanked Stone and gave him his contact details, so Paul could coordinate with the backup personnel when he headed over to the nursery himself.

But, first, he wanted to catch up with Slade. It had been a while since Paul had seen his old friend, and Paul hoped Slade would be able to tell him more about the local talent. Werewolves were a known quantity to Paul, but he still had many questions about Lance. He wasn't sure Slade would give him answers, but he at least had to try. One thing he knew for certain—Slade would not lead him astray.

By his very nature, Slade was a holy man. A shaman. A being close to the spirit world, serving the path of Light in one of the deepest ways possible. Slade was also now mated to a Priestess of the Lady. A more spiritual couple would be hard to find.

When Stone left the office, and it was just Lance, Slade and Paul left, things got quiet. Paul would have left, but Slade motioned for him to stay and took a strategic spot between Paul and Lance.

"I didn't see this coming, but I think it's important that you two meet," Slade began. Paul realized the import of the holy man's words right away. Lance looked a bit more skeptical. "You are both shifters of mythic origins," Slade went on, making Paul shoot him a surprised glance.

"Seriously?" For one breathless moment, Paul got his hopes up, but then, he realized there was no way Lance was a dragon. He just didn't feel that immense. He was just as powerful, but he was something much smaller in scale than a dragon.

"What are you?" Lance asked again, and Paul tried not to take offense.

"That's not normally something people ask," Slade admonished the other man gently. "It's considered impolite in shifter circles, but since you're new to all of this, I suspect my friend, Paul, will cut you some slack." Slade's ghostly blue gaze turned to Paul, seeking his agreement.

Paul shrugged. In the grand scheme of things, getting upset over a few misplaced words wasn't really worth it. "I'll tell if you will," Paul said, using a bit of humor to hopefully diffuse some of the tension.

Lance looked at him warily, then seemed to come to a decision. He nodded his blond head and said just one word. "Phoenix."

Paul didn't understand. Was he talking about where they were? Apparently, his confusion showed on his face because Lance sighed and clarified.

"I am a phoenix shifter."

"No shit?" Paul wasn't quite shocked. This, after all, would explain part of Syd's visions. "She saw a phoenix and a dragon," Paul murmured, then spoke in a stronger voice. "I am a dragon shifter. The only one I know of. I am looking for my kin, if any still live."

In for a penny, in for a pound. That was the saying, he thought. Paul figured, if Lance knew of any dragons around, he might be willing to share that information, now that they were establishing trust between them.

"I take it the woman you're protecting is the one having visions?" Slade asked, his gaze filled with interest.

"Yeah. Syd has started having visions, and they include both dragon fire and phoenix wings. She wasn't sure what she was seeing. I think she still believes it's some sort of metaphor, but considering the two of us..." Paul motioned toward Lance and then himself. "Well, I think what she's seeing is probably literal."

"I think I may need to talk with her," Slade said, surprising Paul. Slade usually wasn't one to interfere directly, but maybe his mating had changed the reclusive cat.

"I can arrange that. Syd's pretty friendly, and she really wants to know more about her visions. Until recently, she was just a regular human being with no special powers," Paul explained. "This is all very new to her."

"I can understand that," Lance muttered, making Paul look at his sharply, seeking more. Lance sighed and sat heavily back into his desk chair. Lance and Slade sat again in the guest chairs, the meeting reconvening, apparently, with one less member. "I was a regular guy until a few months ago," Lance explained. "Then, all this phoenix stuff started happening, and we got attacked by a *Venifucus* mage and a bunch of her goons. There was a show down right out in the car lot, and all hell broke loose. Then, I...changed...and all of a sudden, I was flying and using this immense power to just turn all the bad guys to ash."

Lance seemed a little shell-shocked still. Paul was aghast that such a fierce magic battle had happened here, and there wasn't the faintest residue that he could detect. That phoenix magic must be potent, indeed.

"Phoenix shifters have many gifts, but being able to see evil and send flames to combat it are among the most powerful. No trace is left behind when a phoenix uses its flame. This entire car lot is testament to that," Slade marveled.

"I can't sense anything of what you say happened here," Paul confirmed. "Even I can't do magic without leaving something behind." He looked at Lance with newfound respect.

"Like dragon shifters, phoenix shifters are nearly immortal compared to human lifespans," Slade went on. "That first shift, though, is a doozy. Legend has it that, if they succumb to the call of the sun during their first shift, the phoenix will consume itself and wait to be reborn."

"I can attest to that, too," Lance said with a rueful shake of his head. "The call of the sun was very powerful, but my mate grounded me, and I was able to make it back to her. If I hadn't had her, though, all bets would have been off, and I probably would've chased the sun until I died. I can see why my kind don't often make it past the first shift."

"And the third most common trait of phoenix shifters is that they are reputed to be able to see the future," Slade said in a quiet voice, which made both of the other men look at him.

"Not another one?" Lance said, his words making Paul frown. Another what? Another phoenix?

Slade held up his hands palms outward. "I'm not saying she is, but I'm also not willing to say she isn't." Slade turned his gaze to Paul. "Lance isn't the only phoenix shifter to earn his wings lately. There's another. A female. And, though this kind of thing is incredibly rare, there have been signs all over the world lately that the side of Light is gearing up for a major battle. Rumors abound about the return of Elspeth the Destroyer to the mortal realm. If she really has come back, it makes sense to me that the most magical beings on the side of good would be awakening in response. Lance could've gone the rest of his life without his phoenix spirit coming to the fore, yet now, in less than a year, not one, but two phoenixes have manifested here, in this place." Slade looked from Paul to Lance and back again. "And then, you show up."

"Syd saw dragons. More than just me. A cavern full of sleeping dragons," Paul admitted.

Slade slapped his hands down on his jeans-clad thighs.

"Well, doesn't that just beat all?" he asked rhetorically. "Two—maybe three—phoenixes and a passel of dragons. Fasten your seatbelts, boys. I think we're in for a wild ride."

Paul spent another few minutes talking with Slade and Lance. He received a text during that time from Stone, who had gone himself to watch over the nursery. Stone said he'd already laid eyeballs on Syd and was keeping track of her from afar, awaiting further instructions. Paul told the werewolf Alpha to sit tight. He'd meet up with him within the hour.

Paul made the executive decision to invite Slade over for dinner that night. He'd learned that Slade's priestess wife had stayed home in Las Vegas, so the holy man was riding solo. Declining to go to Syd's home, possibly drawing more attention to her, Slade suggested dining together elsewhere. At that point, Lance got into the act, issuing the invitation for them all to have dinner at his house.

After deciding on a time and receiving directions, Paul took his leave of the two men. He got into the borrowed car and headed for the nursery. Every moment away from Syd weighed on his nerves. Was she really some kind of un-hatched phoenix? Paul had no way of knowing for sure, but the possibilities had his head spinning.

When he pulled in to the huge parking lot in front of the nursery, he chose an out-of-the-way spot to one side of the big lot. He spotted Stone when the man peeked out from his observation point and waved Paul over. He'd chosen to sit at a picnic table under a tree that provided good camouflage despite the fact that the seating area had been designed for patrons of the nursery to access a small snack bar on the side of the building.

The main selling point of the picnic area in Paul's mind was the excellent view it gave them of the nursery yard and the pretty woman who worked there, watering plants, pruning them and generally giving them all her attention. Syd seemed oblivious to the fact that she was under close observation, though she looked up when Paul approached the picnic area, and their eyes met across the distance that separated them, whittling it down to nothing. Or, at least, that's how it felt.

Syd felt a tingling awareness run down her spine the moment before she looked up and saw sexy Paul walking across the parking lot toward the picnic area. There was a side entrance to the nursery yard that allowed visitors to access the snack bar, which was most popular when they had events going on but was mostly empty now. As she met Paul's gaze, time seemed to stand still for one breathless moment before picking up the pace once more and marching on.

Paul walked confidently toward a picnic table by a giant old oak, and she realized there was a man already sitting there. Paul nodded to the other man and sat down with him, speaking in a low voice that she couldn't hear from this distance. It looked like they knew each other. Maybe this strange man was part of the backup team Paul had mentioned. If so, they'd come through very quickly. It wasn't even lunch time yet.

Thinking about it, she decided she'd go out to join Paul when it came time for lunch. For now, she had to do some work with the bushes and trees on the back lot. They needed a bit of work before they could be put out on display for sale, which was one of the jobs she most enjoyed. With a little wave and smile, she headed for the supply shed and then made her way around to the private area of the nursery where stock was brought in from the fields and prepped for sale.

The area she needed to work in today was at the farthest edge of the property. She took a pair of large shears and some other supplies she'd need to prune the various trees and shrubs that had recently been brought in from the growing fields. Nobody else was around, which was normal for this part of the nursery unless field workers were bringing in stock from the farms.

Today, the area was empty of life except for the plants and herself, which was just how Syd liked it. She did some of her best work when it was just her and the greenery, and she knew from past experience that time would fly while she tended to the trees. She really loved this part of her job.

Setting to work, she lost all track of time while inspecting each tree closely. She was so engrossed in the work that the sound of footsteps took her by surprise sometime later. Syd spun around to see who might be coming back here, only to find herself backed into the corner she'd been working in by the appearance of Elliot...and he didn't look friendly.

"You're a pain in the ass, Syd," Elliot began, his voice angry. She knew nobody in the public portions of the nursery would hear them way back here. Even if she screamed, it was unlikely anyone would notice.

"So are you, Elliot." She fought back verbally, knowing it wouldn't do to show weakness to a bully. "You sent people to bug my house! What the hell did you think you were doing?" Better to have it out in the open since he probably knew damned well that she knew it had been him behind the sudden appearance of a goon squad at her home.

"I was thinking we could work together, but now that you've brought in your bodyguards, plans have changed." He walked closer, picking up her long shears as he went. Those things were designed for trimming bushes and had foot-long blades that she, herself, had sharpened just that morning. A formidable weapon.

"Whose plans?" she asked, even as she backed away as much as she could. She was truly trapped now, between a dense wall of trees that had been piled on one side and a tall security fence on the other. Elliot was blocking the only escape route.

"Mine," he answered shortly, clearly enraged. "And my master's. You were going to be my ticket up the hierarchy. If I could deliver your untrained power to my master, I would have been richly rewarded. As it stands, if you can't be recruited, you'll have to be retired. Permanently. Can't have rogue powers out there interfering with our plans."

Retired permanently? That didn't sound good.

"I'm not a power. I'm not anything. I'm just a woman

trying to make a living, and you're having delusions of grandeur!" she shouted at him, even as she felt a tingling heat building in her core. Fight or flight? No. This felt different. More like *fight and fry*...

"Something's happening," Paul said, standing from the picnic table as Stone followed a beat behind.

"What is it?" Stone asked, ready for action immediately, proving his worth as backup. Paul was grateful the man was here, though it was clear he wasn't attuned to Syd yet and didn't feel the buildup of magical power taking place somewhere...in the back of the property.

"Not sure. Follow me," Paul instructed, already going around to the back of the fenced-in property. He'd have to deal with the fence, but it wasn't that high. He could probably jump over it if he couldn't find a gate to open.

Stone was right behind him when Paul felt the energies ratchet upward by a phenomenal degree. Syd was in danger, and something powerful was gathering around her. Whether it was her own magic or someone else's, he couldn't yet be sure.

He caught sight of a man through the bars of the tall fence. He was holding a pair of long metal clippers that gleamed sharply in the sun. His stance was threatening as he waved the tool like a weapon toward where a clearly frightened Syd was standing.

She had one arm outstretched, and Paul could see the glow of her magic manifesting at the tips of her fingers. She was shouting at the man to stay away, and it looked to Paul like her magic was the only thing keeping the aggressive man at bay. It was working, but the guy was fighting Syd's shielding magic, encroaching by slow degrees.

Shit!

Paul looked for a gate. He had to get in there and help her!

CHAPTER 9

"You stay away from me!" Syd shouted at Elliot. She had nowhere to run. Elliot was in a rage like she'd never seen before. He had her death in his eyes, and she was certain he'd stab her with the clippers given half a chance.

Then, something really weird happened. As she threw her hand out to stop him, little blips of red sparkles came out of her fingertips and seemed to hit Elliot in the chest, stopping his forward motion. Was this magic? Was it helping her keep him away? If so, she wanted it to keep on working, but Elliot was fighting back.

"Your untrained magic won't stop me, bitch. And your old friend up in the mountains won't last long after my brothers get through with him," Elliot sneered.

Syd's mind spun into panic. Was he talking about Arthur? Was Arthur under threat in his home, even as she was being attacked here at work?

She could see Elliot struggle for every inch of ground as he moved closer. His forward motion had slowed to a crawl, but he was still moving. Still drawing near. If something didn't change quickly, he'd be in range to hurt her. Damn.

Syd started to panic in earnest. She was trapped, and there was no way around Elliot in the narrow aisle between the densely packed trees. Hysteria rose…along with something else. Something fiery. Something that tingled and made it feel like bubbles were popping against her skin. Frothy bubbles of fire that couldn't hurt her, but would help stop Elliot, she hoped.

She reached out with her hand again and ordered him in her strongest voice. "Go away!"

And then, something happened. The little red sparkles coalesced into a ball of orange fire that formed at the tips of her fingers and then flew at Elliot so fast he couldn't duck. One minute, he was there. The next, the sharp shears were clattering to the pavement, and Elliot was gone.

Holy fuck. What had she just done?

Paul felt the surge of magic before he saw the fireball. He was already halfway over the fence when Syd let loose. Paul expected carnage and flames all over the place. Instead, he watched something he'd never seen before. A fireball that consumed only the man it was aimed at, then disappeared.

Paul dropped down to the other side of the tall fence and looked at the pile of ash that was quickly scattering in an unseen wind. That was all that remained of the man who had threatened Syd. Paul looked up to meet her eyes to find she was truly aghast at what she had done. She was looking from her hand to the ashes, her eyes wide, her body shaking.

"Looks like we've got another one," Stone muttered from the other side of the fence, where he was watching the byplay. Paul turned to him.

"You've seen this before?" Paul asked tersely. Stone nodded.

"Oh, yeah. That, my friend, was phoenix fire. It only burns evil and leaves no trace." Paul looked back to find the little pile of ashes was gone completely. All evidence of the man who had been standing there moments before was gone.

"Syd?" Paul began, walking toward her. "You okay?"

She met his gaze, shock still prevalent in her expression. "What just happened? Did I kill Elliot?"

"That was Elliot?" Paul asked, realizing what must have

happened now that he knew the identity of the man who had cornered her.

She nodded, and Paul closed the distance between them, taking her into a sheltering hug. She melted against him as if he was the only safe place in a storm of confusion.

"*Dragostea mea...*" The Romanian endearment just slipped out. He wondered if she would be upset to hear him call her his love after only one night together. "This is why he was bothering you. Your power is just starting to rise, and they wanted to turn it to evil. You were right to resist, and if Elliot had not been evil, he would not have been affected by your fire. You could be a force for good in the world. He would have tried to warp your strength toward evil. You did the right thing."

"But I'm going to get arrested for murder!" She clutched at his shirt, truly upset while Paul tried not to see the humor in her situation.

He looked over her head at Stone, who didn't bother to hide the smile on his face. Paul jerked his head, a silent order for the other man to move away and keep watch. After a moment, Stone complied.

"You won't be arrested. There is no evidence. Your coworker will have simply disappeared, and nobody but us will ever know what truly happened to him." He tried to find the right words to calm her worries.

"That's awful," she mumbled against his chest. "How could I have done something like that? I didn't want to kill him. Just make him go away."

"He went away, all right," Paul muttered before thinking better of it. Syd stiffened in his arms and moved away.

"What if I lose my temper and do it again? What if I accidently did that to you?" She was upset, and he feared he'd only made it worse with his off-hand comment. He had to try to fix this.

"You wouldn't be able to turn me to ash, Syd. For one thing, I'm not evil. Your special flame only burns evil, which is a good thing, or all these lovely trees and your employer's fine building would be going up in flames right now."

Syd looked around her, realization dawning, it seemed. "Those flames should have spread," she murmured. "Even with the living trees, there's plenty of dry fuel here to take a spark."

"Exactly," Paul agreed. "Your flame is magical. It only attacks evil. Elliot had to have been pure evil to go up so fast."

"He was going to kill me with the shears," she confirmed, nodding toward the metal tool on the ground. "He said, if they couldn't recruit me, they were going to retire me permanently."

"Then, you were right to kill him." Paul didn't sugarcoat his words. She would have to learn to deal with her power now that it was blossoming. "His words betrayed his allegiance. He was part of the *Venifucus*. An order dedicated to pure evil. I shudder to think what they would have done to you to get at your power." He stepped closer to her, catching her gaze. "You did the right thing."

He held her for a long moment while Stone scouted the area. So far, no one had seen a thing. Paul wanted to keep it that way.

"How did you get over the fence?" Syd drew away, her glance going from Paul to the tall fence and back again as she seemed to settle down a bit.

"I'm a shifter. We can do things that mere mortals can't." His smile was meant to tease, and she seemed to respond, the light coming back into her eyes slowly.

"What about him?" She nodded toward Stone, who was just visible in the distance. Stone could probably still hear their conversation, though. Werewolves had excellent hearing. "Isn't he a shifter, too?"

Paul moved back and turned to contemplate Stone, giving Syd a moment to collect herself. "Different species. Wolves aren't very good at climbing, though they can jump pretty well—within reason. That fence has to be ten feet at least. It's probably a bit beyond our new friend's abilities."

Stone threw him a dirty look over his shoulder, proving to Paul that the werewolf Alpha could, indeed, hear him. Paul grinned. Stone probably could've made the leap over the fence, but he'd held back in his role as rear guard. Paul knew that, but he couldn't resist checking if the wolf had a sense of humor.

"I think it's twelve feet, actually," Syd put in. "Howard— the owner—was really proud of it when it was installed. He'd had some trouble with kids getting in back here and messing with the trees in the past, but that ended as soon as the fence went up."

"He didn't put in any surveillance cameras, did he?" Paul felt reasonably sure that there were no electronic gizmos in the area. Most gave off a high-pitched frequency that he could hear, but that went beyond human capabilities. He didn't hear anything like that in the area, but Syd would probably know if there was a recording somewhere he'd have to destroy.

"No. Howard doesn't believe in spying. The fence did the trick, and that was good enough for him," Syd said with quiet authority. Howard sounded like a good boss. At least, Syd's tone when she talked about the man was filled with respect and friendship. "Oh, no," she gasped and stood rigidly upright. "Elliot said something about Arthur being in danger. I have to go help him!"

"Your friend, the shaman?" Paul asked, not having heard all of what Elliot had said to her.

"Elliot said something about his brothers and that Arthur wouldn't last long against them."

"*Venifucus,*" Paul spat. "They must have gone after your friend. They like to destroy those who fight on the side of Light whenever they can. It's part of their plan for total world domination."

"We can't let them hurt Arthur!" Syd pushed past Paul, not bothering to pick up the long shears that had been left on the ground where they fell. He didn't blame her. She probably didn't want to touch anything Elliot had handled.

"Go around front. I'll meet you there with the car," Paul told her before he jumped over the fence.

Seeing Paul's move, Stone came back to meet up with him. The werewolf Alpha offered to follow them up into the mountains right then and there, but Paul declined.

"If you can get a group together—say a half-dozen members of your Pack, or some of the bears—" Paul told Stone as they made their way swiftly back to the parking area, "—we may need some help in the aftermath. Or, if I can't contain them myself, I'd appreciate being avenged, though I don't think it's going to come to that." Paul's dry humor brought a smile to the werewolf Alpha's face. Stone *did* have a sense of humor, after all.

Stone agreed with Paul's request and quickly took note of the directions Paul gave him. Paul knew where Arthur's house was from his aerial reconnaissance the night before. He'd seen the old house, standing proud and lonely on an outcropping of rock midway up a mountain. It had been the only logical place Syd could have come from in her little car.

Stone promised to bring a crew with him as quickly as possible. They'd be right behind Paul and Syd, or so the Alpha claimed. Paul was glad of the promised help. He wasn't sure what they would find when they reached Arthur's house. He also wasn't sure how Syd's fledgling magic would react to another threat. All Paul knew was that he had to help her. He had to help this friend of hers that meant so much to her.

And part of his mission in life was to stop the *Venifucus* wherever and whenever he found them. It was part of his service to the Lady of Light. Part of his calling. Part of his penance for a misspent youth when he wasn't sure which way to go. He'd been tempted into doing some bad things for which he'd atoned long ago, but in his heart, he would never be able to fully cleanse his soul. Thus, he'd struck a deal with the Goddess. He would serve Her and do all in his power to fight the darkness that threatened the mortal realm. In return, someday, perhaps, She would help him forgive himself for his youthful foolishness, and maybe…just maybe…She would help him find his family.

Syd did her best to calm down before she reached the office area. She went straight to the locker room where she retrieved her bag and put away her garden apron and rubber boots. She then went to Howard's office and did the best acting job she could manage under the circumstances, telling her boss she really needed the afternoon off. Howard was a very reasonable fellow, and Syd had been an exemplary employee to this point. She almost never called in sick, and she'd never before left in the middle of the day, so Howard believed her when she said she wasn't feeling well and needed to go home.

He told her to take it easy and feel better. Just like that, she was free to go. Syd clocked out and headed for the parking lot. Paul, thankfully, hadn't moved her car from where he had parked it, and she was able to get in on the driver's side and pull away without anyone seeing him, seated low on the passenger side.

She was glad he hadn't tried to take over. She wouldn't have been able to sit still in the passenger seat for the long drive up into the mountains. As it was, worry was her near-constant companion as she drove them hastily out of town. There would be no stops on the way, this time. No, this was a possible rescue mission. She didn't have time—more importantly, Arthur didn't have time—for her to make her way lazily up the mountain. She had to get there as fast as she could this time and hope for the best.

"Do you want to talk about it?" Paul asked quietly once they'd been on the highway for a few minutes.

"About what? Elliot? Arthur?" she asked, her voice a little shrill even to her own ears. A lot had happened, and she was barely keeping it together.

"All of it," Paul replied patiently. "Any of it," he went on. "I know it's a lot to take in and deal with. You've just discovered you have a potent, sometimes dangerous magic. I know from personal experience how hard that is to understand, at first."

"Personal experience?" she asked, keeping her eyes on the road for the most part, but shooting him a curious glance, now and again.

Paul wanted to tell her the whole story, but she was already overloaded from everything that had happened in the short time since they'd met. He would share only as much as he thought would help her. Feeding her the information a little bit at a time had to be better than bombarding her with all the facts at once, right? He hoped he'd chosen the right strategy.

"I was raised in an orphanage," he reminded her. "I thought I was completely human until I hit puberty, and suddenly, my abilities started to emerge. The day I first shifted was the day I left the orphanage for good. I was fourteen. I've been making my way on my own ever since, learning about what I could do through trial and error."

"But you know other shifters, right? Couldn't they help you?" she asked, her tone sympathetic.

He shook his head. "Different species have different issues. Some cat shifters, for example, start shifting when they're babies. Wolves don't start shifting until puberty, like me, but I'm not a wolf, and very little else of their lore applies to my kind. Bears are close—they're very magical—but not an exact match either. Besides, I didn't meet my first bear shifter until I was in my twenties. By then, I'd figured out most of it." He sighed. "Having the power to hurt and kill was something I didn't deal with well at the time. I was sorely tempted to go too far, to seek revenge on those who had hurt me in the past. And, I'm sorry to say, I gave into the temptation once too often when I was too young to really understand the ramifications of my actions. I have spent most of my adult life trying to make up for my past transgressions," he admitted.

Silence reigned for the next few minutes as Syd got all she could have of the little car's engine. Light as it was, it really moved on the highway, reaching speeds well over the limit, but Syd didn't seem to care, and fortunately—or perhaps, magically—there were no police cars in sight. At this rate, they would make it from the city to the base of the mountains in record time.

"I get feelings about people," Syd told him out of the blue sometime later. "From almost the moment we met, I sensed you were a good person. I wouldn't have let you into my car if I didn't have a good instinct about you." She glanced at him for a moment, compassion in her gaze. "Whatever you did in the past, you've made up for it in the present, and I suspect, you've changed your ways and chosen your path for all time."

Paul was a little stunned by her words but couldn't find any fault with them. She was right. He'd chosen his path. He wasn't going to make the same mistakes he'd made as a young man. He was playing strictly on the side of Light, forevermore. It pleased him down to his soul that she had seen that about him. Most people he encountered weren't so sure of his intentions and tended to mistrust him.

Yet Syd, with so much on the line, had chosen to see only the good in him. It meant a lot. More than it probably should have, so soon into their acquaintance. But who was he to question Fate? Or, perhaps, it was the hand of the Lady, playing out once again in his life.

"You're right about me," he said quietly. "And I have feelings about you, too. Your soul is pure and unblemished. And, regardless of what happened earlier today, it remains so. You did the right thing with Elliot, even though it might take some time for your human half to come to terms with it."

"Human half?" She looked at him, frowning.

"*Dragostea mea*, I'm willing to bet that you're a shifter," he told her. "And, if you are, you will be learning the truth of it sooner rather than later. The only advice I can give you is to not fight the change when you feel it come on. It is what has always been meant to be. Go with it. But remember to come back. My heart will break if you are lost to the shift and do not return to me."

That was about as close as he could come to admitting the deep feelings in his heart for her right now. He didn't want to scare her off by speaking of his love too soon, but he also didn't want her thinking that they had no attachment. Especially since, after speaking with Lance and Slade, he knew her first shift was going to be risky for many reasons. Most importantly, to him, was the chance that she would chase the sun and never return to him. He wanted to impress upon her now that he would be devastated if that were to happen.

At the same time, he couldn't just come out and tell her she was a phoenix. No, that was still just an educated guess at the moment. She could turn out to be something entirely different. He didn't want to build up any expectations. He had to let the process unfold naturally and see where it led.

"This is all just too weird," she said, shaking her head in denial.

"Forget it for now," he counseled. "Let's just take this one step at a time. We'll check on your friend, Arthur, and see what happens from there, okay?"

She breathed deep before nodding agreement. "That sounds like a plan to me," she said as they neared the foot of the mountains which could be seen in the near distance. Clouds were gathering around the peaks and rapidly descending.

"Strange weather pattern forming above," he noted, gesturing skyward. He thought he knew what the gathering storm meant, but he didn't say anything just yet. He knew he would feel it the moment magical energy began to fly and then...so would he.

Syd grew more anxious the closer they got to the mountains. As she drove, she began to see things. It wasn't a full-fledged vision, or she'd have been in trouble since she was behind the wheel, but she saw events—future events, she somehow knew—overlay the view of the road in front of her.

She watched as events played out. Arthur was surrounded by people. She recognized some of them from those who had been in her house, planting bugs and cameras. Bad guys. But there was one... Someone new. Someone powerful. Someone the rest deferred to, as if he was in charge.

That man faced Arthur, and then, bright light flared and blocked out her view. The vision ended, and she knew they had little time.

"Darnit," she muttered as her vision cleared.

"What?" Paul was attentive, though he had shown he was willing to let her lead this posse, which she appreciated.

"Arthur is going to be surrounded by people. I recognized some of them from the house, but there's a new guy. A leader. Someone who can lob brightly pulsing balls of energy." She reached for words to describe what she'd seen but found it hard. "I don't know how to explain it. It looked really dangerous, and they were all focused on Arthur. I'm worried."

She said nothing more as she navigated the off-ramp that led to the small road that corkscrewed up the mountain. About halfway up, hidden by the curvature of the mountain itself, was the outcropping on which Arthur's house stood.

"Stop the car."

"What?" She looked over at Paul, shocked by the order in his voice.

"I feel the magic gathering," he told her. She felt the tingling energy in the air, too, but wasn't altogether sure what it was. Paul seemed certain. "I can get to your friend faster than the car. I'll go help him."

"How?" she asked, even as she stopped the car in the middle of the empty road. Even in the middle of the day, this road was seldom traveled.

Paul got out and stepped back away from the car, even as he held her gaze. "I can fly," he told her calmly before his form was engulfed by darkly sparkling energy. A moment later, an honest-to-goodness dragon stood in the middle of the road.

"Holy shit," she breathed, her mouth agape. Paul seemed to grin a split second before he launched himself skyward, shooting like a rocket upward into the darkening clouds.

She got the car going again, her hands trembling the tiniest bit. She'd seen some weird shit lately, but that had been in visions—not reality. Now, her visions were coming true, and she didn't know if she was ready for it to be real.

Whether she was ready or not, though, things were happening, and people were in danger. She had to get to Arthur. She knew Paul would do his best to help protect her friend, but she also—somehow—knew that she had to be there. She didn't know why or what she could do to help, but she knew, in her heart of hearts, that she had to be present.

Maybe Paul's presence would stall things long enough for her to get there. Heaven knew, a dragon had to give any sane person pause. Of course, that was relying on the sanity of bad guys who served some sort of evil super-being. Who said *they* were sane?

CHAPTER 10

Paul flew through the clouds, feeling the malevolent magic gathering. He knew where Arthur's house was thanks to his previous flight in the area, but the house was hidden from the road by the shape of the mountain, which was a bit craggy. Whatever was going on at Arthur's wouldn't be seen except from someone higher up the mountain—if there were any people up there—or from the air. From below, even a magical light show wouldn't be seen by the casual observer.

And with the thick covering of dark clouds, the camouflage was even better. These were no ordinary clouds. Paul could feel them pulling at his wings, trying to ground him. They pulsed with evil, the whispers of angry chanting and hastily cast repulsion spells bounced off his slick hide. Whoever was up there casting, they were no match for a dragon.

He hoped that continued to be the case, but he wouldn't know until he got up there. It took longer than it should have because of the magical fog that tried to delay him, but eventually, he broke through to the area he'd seen from above where Arthur lived. He set down on the edge of the flat area in front of the main house. It looked like that was the center of the action.

Paul took in the scene quickly. An old Native American

man was standing in the center of a ring of people who were chanting. It was they who had called the dark fog, but it wasn't getting anywhere near the old man. Rather, he seemed to be repelling it with no effort at all, which was why it was spilling down the side of the mountain.

Behind the ring of people—some of whom Paul recognized as having been part of the group in Syd's house—was vehicle, just pulling up. At the wheel, was the leader of the group that had tried to bug Syd's home. He got out and ran around to the back-passenger-side door of the big car that had tinted windows and every luxury add-on. He opened the door, and another man stepped out.

This was the power, Paul realized. The real mage had arrived. The minions had just been sent ahead to occupy the old man until the big gun could get here. It looked like Paul had arrived just in time. And, thanks to the dark fog, nobody seemed to realize he was even there yet. His dark scales blended well with the dark smoky fog. They didn't see him, but that would all change the moment he stepped closer. Then, he thought, things would really start happening.

Syd pushed her little car as fast as she dared up the winding two-lane road that led to Arthur's. She saw the roiling black mist sliding down the mountain, and it sickened her. There was something really wrong there. Something...evil.

But she didn't know what she could do to fix it. Her best bet was to get up to Arthur's and see if she could help him directly. Maybe he'd know what to do about the oily black smoke oozing down the mountain. Arthur knew all sorts of things. She'd bet he'd know what to do about that, too.

Paul was up there, too, by now. She worried about him. She'd only known him a short time, but so much had happened during those precious hours. He'd become special to her. A lifeline in a turbulent time...and so much more. She wondered if he was in her life to stay or just passing through. He said some things, sometimes, that made her start to believe that maybe he was thinking about the future. A future with her.

Every moment she was with him, everything just felt so right. From the way he'd helped her to his tender lovemaking. He'd been alternately gentle and demanding with her, and she'd loved every minute of it. He'd given her what she needed, when she needed it, almost as if he could read her mind when they were in bed together. That was something she'd never experienced before, and she wanted more of it. More of him. Forever, if he'd let her.

Like so many things lately, she wasn't sure how she knew being with Paul was the right thing. She just knew it was. She also knew she would welcome him into her life—into her bed—for as long as he wanted to be there. She only prayed he wanted to stay forever.

They'd only spent one night together, and in the normal way of things, it was probably way too soon to be thinking about sharing their lives forever, but that's where her mind had gone all day. She couldn't seem to help herself. When she'd been trying to focus on the work she loved, instead, she'd been daydreaming of what it would be like to be married to Paul, to spend the rest of her days with him and have babies that looked like miniature versions of him and her. She'd been sort of giddy all morning…until the showdown with Elliot had changed everything.

Paul had been there when she'd needed him again. Her knight in invisible armor, leaping to her rescue yet again. He hadn't fought her battle this time, but he'd definitely helped her in the aftermath. She wasn't entirely sure she could've handled the emotional fallout from what she'd done without him.

She still wasn't sure she was okay with what had happened to Elliot, but some new instinct inside her was almost purring with satisfaction. She wasn't sure she liked that response. She abhorred violence and especially killing, but she also despised evil, and the fight with Elliot had really been self-defense, when it came down to it. She didn't see, now, how it could have turned out any other way, and she was trying hard to accept the new feelings that the encounter had awoken.

There was satisfaction, yes…but above all, there was a new feeling of justice having been served. Somehow, she knew deep inside, that she'd been the instrument of justice. It was a deep *knowing*. A certainty. Though, again, where it had come from, she had no idea.

Her thoughts were scattered as she raced up the side of the mountain as fast as she dared. A million thoughts jumbled together, running through her mind as she rounded curve after curve, zigzagging her way up the side of the craggy mountain as dark mist descended. Luckily, the darkness was concentrated on the side of the mountain, away from the road, but that was also a problem, because that's where Arthur's house was located. Whatever that evil-feeling darkness was, it was coming from Arthur's.

Syd prayed as she pushed her car nearer and nearer, taking the curvy road as fast as she dared, but it was still too far. Whatever was going on up there, she hoped Arthur—and now Paul—could hold on a little longer. She had no idea what she could do to help, but there was that *knowing* again, that said she could definitely do *something*. She'd turned Elliot to ash, after all. Perhaps she could harness that energy again and help stop the bad guys who were threatening her friend.

He was just an old man. What had he ever done to deserve this? Syd felt intense guilt over the idea that these bastards were harassing Arthur because she had befriended him. If she was the cause of all this bother, she would feel even worse than she did already. She had to apologize to Arthur—if they all lived through whatever was going on up there.

As the sorcerer stepped out of the showy car, he began to wave his hands around in the air. Paul watched from the shadows. He'd pick his time to appear. For now, he wanted to see what he might be up against. The old man looked to be holding his own easily, in no danger from the B team the *Venifucus* had sent ahead to harry the old fellow.

Paul wasn't impressed by the show the mage was putting on. All that flailing about with his arms might look dramatic, but it was really a waste of energy. The really strong mages didn't need to make all that fuss to get things done. That led Paul to believe that, while the enemy might be powerful, he wasn't among the elite the *Venifucus* had in their number. Probably someone trying to work his way up the ladder of evil. Well, his journey to the top of that particular dastardly brotherhood was about to come to an abrupt end if Paul had anything to say about it.

It was as the sorcerer began to gather his dark power that Paul first scented blood. That changed things. The man who had arrived in the swanky car was a blood path mage. Evil incarnate, as far as Paul was concerned.

Those who followed the blood path took their power by force from those they preyed upon. The ultimate rush for them was killing, but they were also known to capture and imprison those whose power was just starting to emerge. Like Syd. This bastard was probably in town because of her. Lured here by the promise of a young power to dominate, incarcerate, and bleed off little by little through use of torture and agony.

Syd would not suffer that fate, Paul vowed. Nor would any other innocent suffer it at the hands of this blood path mage. His reign of infamy would end here. Today.

As Paul gathered himself to step forward, out of the shadows, something happened. The old man at the center of the circle began to glow bright with the power that was his to command. Paul hadn't really expected much, not knowing Arthur personally, but Syd had said the old guy was a *retired* shaman. Paul had known, from the moment Syd had said those words, that there was something a little off about the claim of retirement.

Shaman didn't just retire. Holy men and women remained true to their calling all their lives, and a little thing like old age seldom slowed them down. Paul had been impressed by Arthur's abilities to this point, but what he saw now made him hold back from revealing his presence. He'd be better off as the ace in the hole. Arthur wasn't doing too badly at the moment, and Paul wanted to see how it would play out.

The instant Arthur got in trouble, however, Paul would break cover and go to his aid. He wasn't interested in seeing Syd's friend hurt.

At that moment, the old shaman seemed to look directly into Paul's eyes before the glow about his person intensified. Arthur knew Paul was there. Paul didn't question how he knew that, but he did. Just as he knew the kind of power Arthur had at his command.

It was a familiar power. A power laced with the taste of the Mother of All. The Lady of Light. The Goddess Paul served. As did Arthur, apparently.

As Paul watched, Arthur's image was superimposed by a glowing outline of translucent ceremonial garb. This was the shaman in all his glory, robed and beaded and feathered, dressed in the tools of his trade.

In a split second, Paul realized what he was seeing. It was a spectacle he'd seen only once before, many thousands of miles away from here, under very different circumstances, but Paul readily recognized a being who had pledged his life to the Goddess. Regardless of the lack of traditional armor, Paul knew Arthur was a Knight of the Light. A warrior pledged to fight on the side of Light against evil wherever and whenever he encountered it.

He was, indeed, a holy man. More than that, he was a *blessed* man. For only rare beings were chosen by Her to serve Her in this fashion. That Syd's friend was a Knight was surprising, but Paul supposed he should have expected something like this. It was clear Syd's path had been guided...guarded...by those who wanted to see her develop into the warrior for Light he knew she could be. It all seemed so clear now.

As the sorcerer began to gather power, Arthur began a chant in his Native tongue. The forces of Light and dark began to swirl around the circle formed by the *Venifucus* stooges. There were a lot of them and only one old man— albeit a Knight of the Light—to fight against them. Paul stepped out of the dissipating fog and into the clear area.

And then, there were two to face the *Venifucus* gang.

Syd rounded the last bend and then took the turn-off that was Arthur's driveway. It was a dirt road, well, sort of a stone road, that snaked around the side of the mountain, into the crag that hid Arthur's home from view of the main road. Syd had to slow down because the road was narrow and winding, but her anxiety was at an all-time high. What was going on? Was Arthur okay? Was Paul okay? She almost dreaded what she might find around the next bend.

And then, she saw a glowing light burning away that sickly dark fog that had been dripping down the mountain. It was daytime. The darkness was unnatural. Even she—unversed in the ways of magic—had seen that.

But something was fighting back now, dissipating the scary darkness. She took that to be a good sign as she rounded the last bend. She saw Arthur's little house, perched on the side of the mountain, with the big space in back that was a flattened section of the outcrop that then dropped off the side of the mountain. There was a fancy car parked in her way, so Syd stopped her own car in the middle of the driveway. They'd blocked her, so she didn't feel any guilt over blocking them in return.

Besides, nobody she knew had money for a car like that, except maybe Howard, who owned the nursery. But he wasn't a frivolous guy. He'd rather have a handy new pickup truck than a car that was just for show and couldn't carry a load. She marveled that the expensive machine had even made it up Arthur's dirt road in the first place.

Looking beyond the annoying car, Syd noted the gathering in the flat area adjacent to Arthur's home. Paul—in dragon form—was there, as was Arthur. Even as she watched, half of the circle of people who had been surrounding Arthur broke away and went to face Paul. He was on the far side of the clearing, near where the mountain dropped off down the slope. He must have landed there.

Syd just shook her head at the idea that she was looking at a real, live dragon. If she hadn't seen Paul shapeshift right in front of her eyes, she wouldn't have believed it possible, but there he was, a dark, midnight blue dragon, facing a half dozen jerks who were chanting some nonsensical gibberish that Syd didn't like. What little she could hear of it sounded mean spirited. Evil, even.

Her gaze tracked to Arthur, standing tall and firm against a man in an expensive suit who was waving his arms like some kind of circus performer. Ignoring that weirdness for now, she noted the man who had bashed her over the head standing to the other guy's right. How dare he show his face here? She had a bone to pick with that asshole, and she was just in the mood to punch him in the face.

Flanking them were four more people, chanting like the others, and watching the arm-waving guy for instructions—or so it appeared to Syd. She thought she recognized some of the faces of the chanters as people who'd been part of the team that had raided her house, and her anger grew. How dare they?

"You know you cannot win, shaman," the arm-waver shouted, everything stalling out for a few minutes. The chanters stopped chanting, and everyone waited to see what was going to happen now that the head guy had started talking.

"You attack me on my home territory," Arthur said quietly, with ancient dignity. "It is you who cannot win. Not here. Not now. Not ever."

"What if I appealed to your ally?" The nattily dressed man turned his conniving gaze to Paul. "Oh, dragon," he singsonged, "what if I could give you your heart's desire?"

Paul stilled, and all motion around him ceased as the half-dozen goons who had kept him at bay watched their leader attentively. Paul shimmered, shifting shape so that he was human again between one eye blink and the next. He wore different clothing that he'd been wearing in the car, Syd noted with some surprise. Black leather covered him from head to toe as if he'd been riding a motorcycle. He looked badass…and totally sexy.

Syd stayed behind the fancy car, not wanting to draw attention to herself just yet. She wasn't sure what she could contribute to the confrontation, and she didn't feel the buildup of energy she'd felt when confronted by Elliot. Without that, she didn't know if she could do much of anything to help, and she might just get herself hurt or killed. Better she watch and wait for the right opportunity. For now, she was observing, hoping the magic—or whatever it had been—came back to her when, and if, she needed it.

"And just what do you think is my heart's desire?" Paul asked the other man, walking calmly through the line of people who had been fending him off with their chanting—or trying to—only moments before. Paul moved as if he owned the place, walking confidently and with no hurry, toward the man in the suit.

"Come now," the fancy man replied in an oily tone. "I know how rare your kind is. Have you ever even met another dragon shifter?" The man smiled, and it turned Syd's stomach. "I know where there are other dragons. I've even worked with a few. I could introduce you. If…you come to work for me."

Paul seemed to consider, and Syd wanted to gasp, but she didn't dare draw attention to herself. He couldn't seriously be entertaining the idea. No. He had to be playing some sort of game with the guy. No way would Paul turn to evil to achieve his goals. Just. No. Way.

For one fraction of a second, Paul felt temptation, but then, he looked across the yard toward where he knew Syd was hiding behind the car, and all thoughts of taking the easy road fled. The so-called *easy* route to his goals had never proved to be either easy or the actual route to his goals. No way would he make that mistake ever again. But the sorcerer

PHOENIX AND THE DRAGON

didn't know that.

"Work for you?" Paul mused, moving closer to the sorcerer. He wasn't quite in striking distance yet, but he would do his best to put himself between the blood path mage and Syd. Paul couldn't be certain the others hadn't seen her approach and he wanted her covered should they decide to attack her again. "What's the pay? Besides an introduction to other dragons, I mean."

"Pay?" The sorcerer seemed taken aback for a moment before the ingratiating smile returned to his face. "Why, I'm sure we could come to some arrangement. I'm not a poor man, and those who work for me are treated well."

"I'm sure," Paul said, unable to hide the sneer from his voice. Was this guy for real? "Just who would I be working for?"

"I am Samuel Kreegar," he said as if the name should ring a bell. It didn't.

"Should I have heard of you?" Paul asked bluntly. He was almost in position. The sorcerer didn't like Paul's question, but he seemed to hold onto his anger by a very frail edge.

"I am Third Warden of the West Coast Coven. Once I finish here, my elevation to Second is almost guaranteed, which will mean a great deal more power, which will, of course, trickle down to those who work for me." The man couldn't sound any slimier if he tried, but Paul had just learned something about the way the *Venifucus* was organized, so he tried to keep the guy talking, even as he moved into position to block any attack on Syd.

"Coven?" Paul tried to sound casual, even as he questioned the other man. "You mean like for witches?"

Kreegar laughed, and it wasn't a pleasant sound. "Witches…and so much more. The hags are among the weakest of our number," he boasted. "And they talk too much," he finished dismissively. Apparently, Kreegar didn't realize he had a lot in common with the women he despised.

"I just want to be clear," Paul said, finally arriving at the optimum position he'd been seeking. "You're all sworn to the

111

Venifucus, right?"

Kreegar tilted his head. "You know we are. Why ask?"

"I just want to be certain," Paul said, gathering his power for a quick shift. "Before I declare my ongoing allegiance to the Lady of Light." The moment the words left his mouth, he shifted into his much more durable dragon form.

He gathered his breath even as the sorcerer's eyes widened in shock, but Kreegar was quicker than Paul had hoped. He had a shield up around himself and his people even before the first lick of flame blasted from Paul's mouth. The dragon's fire did not touch them, but at least it put them on the defensive. Paul hoped Syd and Arthur would take advantage of the few moments of reprieve he bought them by running for cover.

The moment he ran out of air—and therefore, flame—the fight was on. Kreegar lobbed dark bolts of acidic magic at Paul, but it couldn't penetrate his dragon hide. The scales were tough and protected not only physically, but magically, as well. Still, each hit stung like the dickens as Paul gathered another deep breath for flame.

He looked around to find that Syd had broken cover and raced to Arthur's side. It looked like she was trying to convince Arthur to run away, but the old man was having none of it. As a result, Syd was out in the open, in the midst of it all. Paul didn't like that. No, not at all. There was no guarantee her magic would manifest at the moment she needed it. Just because she'd been able to deal with Elliot, that didn't mean she was ready to deal with a full-out assault by multiple enemies.

Damn. If only she weren't so vulnerable out there in the open like that. Paul wasn't sure what he could do to help aside from keeping the bad guys busy, so he opened his mouth and blew fire at their enemies, doing his best to take the pressure off Syd and Arthur long enough for something to develop in their favor.

With any luck, the wolves would arrive soon. Backup was coming. They just had to hold out long enough for it to get here. That thought firmly in mind, Paul went to work.

That Kreegar guy made Syd's skin crawl. She had been silently rooting for Paul to choose the right side, and when he did, she felt a huge sense of relief and joy. She *knew* he was one of the good guys.

She ran over to Arthur, daring greatly, but when she got to him, he refused to move. He just looked at her with that calm, sort of all-knowing expression in his eyes and stood firm no matter how much she pleaded.

"This is not the time to run," he told her quietly, even as the roaring of flame sounded nearby. "One cannot run in the face of evil. It must be confronted and stopped, or it will take over."

"Arthur, there's a freaking *dragon* buying us time to get away," she told him, trying to reach for his arm but getting nowhere. It was as if there was some kind of invisible force field around Arthur that she couldn't reach through. "Take the gift he's giving you and get to safety."

Arthur just looked at her, his eyes shining with energy she didn't fully understand. "Safety is not what you think it is," he told her. "You must take this moment to reach your full potential. You must find the fire within and let it take flight. Only your flame can end this standoff safely."

"Safely? Arthur, I killed someone today," she admitted, still feeling anxious over what had happened. One side of her felt a sense of calm triumph over besting evil, but the regular human part of her psyche—the only side she'd known until recently—was still shocked and appalled at what she'd done.

"You ended an agent of evil. What you are would not allow you to harm anyone who had not committed their hearts and souls to evil. You are meant to do what you did. You are a tool of the divine. Or, you will be. Once you reach your full potential. Once you take to flight."

"Flight?" She was so confused.

Syd looked around and realized that while Paul was keeping the big bad guy at bay, some of the lesser minions were starting to take note of her presence. Arthur seemed well shielded—whatever that barrier was—from their anger, but she was wide open. A nice, juicy target.

Suddenly, about five of them started chanting again. Shit!

Syd could feel something pressing in on her. It was a force. Something they were doing with their words and their slow movements closer to her. They couldn't get right up in her face because of whatever it was Arthur was doing, but they were definitely inching their way closer. She felt the pressure all around.

Then...something began to tingle inside her. She started to feel hot. An aching fire in her blood made her tear at her clothing, but it was no use. She felt the rise of...whatever that had been...magic, she guessed. The same thing she'd felt at the nursery when Elliot accosted her, but more. Much, much more.

She moved away from Arthur, not wanting to hurt him. Unfortunately, that brought her closer to the minions. She tried to keep an eye on all of them, but they were closing in, and she doubled over in sudden gut-wrenching pain. Something was happening.

Then, there was cold steel against her ribs. She straightened, shocked by the freezing feel of it. The evil feel of it. She came face to face with the bastard that had hit her on the head, and she saw red. Literally. Red.

The red of fire. She realized immediately what the steel was. It was a gun placed against her ribs with icy cold intent. Her skin started to glow, and her temperature rose even higher. Everything shimmered with the heat she was generating.

"Stop it, bitch," the man sneered. "Or I'll shoot you."

She couldn't have stopped what was happening for anything. She didn't know how to control it, and she didn't even really know what it was. Whatever was going to happen was just going to happen no matter what she did. Syd growled at the man, unable to form words as she gave in to the inevitable.

Flame erupted from her. It engulfed her. She heard the gun fire, but she didn't feel the impact. Instead, she felt the cold steel turn hot and molten, and heard the pops as the remaining ammunition baked off, scattering all around, none of it coming even close to her. Somehow, at least one round hit every last one of the minions who had been menacing her and Arthur. They fell to the ground, one by one, as the man who had tried to shoot her began to scream.

She couldn't hear much over the roar of the flames, but she watched as he burned in her flame, sinking down into ashes almost within the blink of an eye. She was glad. He hadn't suffered too much. Her human heart felt bad enough about killing him. She didn't want to make his suffer. She didn't want to take joy in his pain as he would have done with her.

Syd looked at Arthur to make certain his magical shield had held and that he hadn't been hit by any of the wild bullets. He smiled serenely at her, a bit of triumph in his gaze as he motioned toward the sky with the glowing ceremonial staff in his hands.

"Fly, my child. Become what you were meant to be. Fulfill your destiny!"

She just barely heard his words over the roaring of the flames. They were licking out from her fingers, and even as she looked down at her arms, they...changed. Her arms grew feathers and then elongated and spread out into wings.

She had wings? Wings of fire? What the...?

The fire created a sort of wind, and suddenly, she was floating. Then, she was...flying?

It felt natural. It felt right. She wasn't scared of flying. She was only concerned for the people down below, growing smaller as she rose higher.

She could feel it now—the sun was calling her—but Paul and Arthur were down there. Paul was buying time, but Arthur just stood there, shining. He was protected by something she didn't quite understand, but for how long? She had to go back and help them.

Closing her wings in tight to her body, she arrowed down, snapping her wings open at the last moment as she glided over the outcropping. Paul looked up as his flame died out. He was vulnerable, and Kreegar went after him. Paul stumbled backward as blood red energies reached out for him.

Just the sight of those energies sickened her. The newfound part of her that could fly seemed to know what to do, so she let her instincts guide her as she circled and came at the sorcerer from behind this time. She fanned her wings and felt...something...gathering. It was like before with Elliot, only way bigger.

The energy felt enormous, and it couldn't be contained. As she soared over the battleground, she felt it bleeding out the tips of her feathers. Little sparks of fire blanketed the ground below, and she cringed inwardly at the thought that she might be hurting her friends or setting fire to Arthur's house. She looked around as she circled and was grateful to see the house wasn't on fire. Thank goodness!

The minions weren't menacing either Arthur or Paul, anymore. Those who'd been shot by the cooked ammunition either lay where they fell, bleeding, or were crawling away as fast as they could manage. Those who had been with Kreegar, facing Paul, were running, too. They were ducking the flaming sparks, and when one happened to land on them, they howled in pain.

Satisfied she was at least helping in some small way, Syd wheeled around for another pass.

CHAPTER 11

Paul staggered as Kreegar got in a good shot that made him return to human form. How in the world did that bastard manage that one? Paul shook his head. Kreegar had power, Paul would give him that, but they had fought to a standoff. Paul could keep him at bay, but he hadn't found a way to get under Kreegar's defenses yet...but he would.

"You're wasting your power here," Kreegar shouted, his attention split between dodging Syd's phoenix sparks and watching Paul's every move. "There's still time to change your mind. Join me and your brethren. Several dragons are allied with me, and we'll be on the right side of things when the *Mater Priori* makes her presence known to the world."

"The Destroyer was banished long ago," Paul countered, fishing a bit as he looked for an opening. Of course, he was willing to listen to any intel Kreegar was willing to pass on...before he died.

"I have news for you," Kreegar said in a smug tone. "She's back. Has been for months now. She's just recovering from the journey before we make our move. The other dragons in our number are part of a long-term plan we've had for centuries to re-take the world now that our leader is returned. The war is only just starting, my friend. You should think hard about what side you want to be on."

"I'm not your friend, and I've already chosen. Long ago." Paul moved toward Arthur, who was also moving—finally—toward him. They stood, side by side, facing Kreegar.

"That's too bad. I didn't want to have to end you, dragon, but if you will not join us, you will have to die." Kreegar launched his most powerful attack yet, forcing both Paul and Arthur to stumble back a few feet, but Arthur's shields were holding strong around both of them.

Now, in human form, Paul called his magic and began lobbing mage bolts back at Kreegar. Arthur was handling the shields for both of them, allowing Paul time to concentrate on the fight. In human form, Paul's magical bolts took the form of lightning-shaped spears of fire. They stabbed through and burned away the sickly blood red balls of fog that Kreegar sent to envelop and smother Paul and Arthur.

Arthur's light shone through the attack, but his power wasn't infinite. At some point, Kreegar would wear him down, and things would go from bad to worse. Right now, Paul was able to fight without having to worry about shielding, but even so, the best he could do was push back when Kreegar pushed them. They were pretty evenly matched, which meant Kreegar was one of the most powerful mages Paul had ever encountered. He was used to having the advantage over his opponents. This time, it was too close to call, and Kreegar was really making Paul work for every inch of ground he gained.

They exchanged blows for a while, but Syd was circling, and she swooped low for another pass, even though she didn't seem real sure about her power yet. She'd found the phoenix within, but she hadn't yet proved able to harness the reputed power in her new form.

Paul knew it was a lot to ask that she hit the ground running. Or, rather, take to the sky throwing magical fire bolts. She deserved a chance to get used to her new form before having to fight in it, but she wasn't getting it. She had better figure it out pretty quick or Paul wasn't sure what would happen. They needed her at full power on this.

He sensed her swooping around for another pass, but she was approaching from behind Paul and Arthur's position, in full view of Kreegar. Paul wanted to shout when Kreegar's aim went over his head. He was lobbing those balls of blood magic directly into Syd's path.

Shit!

Syd saw the puff of reddish grey smoke heading straight for her. She wasn't good enough with her wings yet to avoid it, though she tried. She hit the sickening miasma head on and squinted her eyes shut, holding her breath until she was clear of it. It had felt sort of like swimming through molasses. She'd lost altitude, as well.

In fact, she would be dangerously close to Kreegar in another moment. *Oh, crap!*

Panic must have triggered something inside her because she felt power rise once more, quickly, and she followed her instincts. She screeched, her voice coming out of her bird's beak unlike anything she'd ever heard before. It was loud, and it was high-pitched, and it was pretty evident that it actually hurt Kreegar.

He didn't just cringe—he fell back under the force of her vocalization. He looked stunned, and she let her newly discovered phoenix side take the reins. Fire surrounded her. It shot from her feathers like big, pointy darts, each swirling in the air on its way to the target: Kreegar.

Tilting her wings experimentally, she learned quickly how to focus the onslaught so that the fire rained down on him—and only him. He didn't just fall back this time. No, he was screaming as he landed on his ass in the dirt, his hands rising up to try to protect himself, but to no avail.

His tattooed face lit up as his shields failed, and then, she was past him, turning tight for another pass. Only…Kreegar was gone. Her flames had overcome the protective properties of his magical tattoos and whatever shields he had and consumed him…and only him. The dry tinder of grasses and scrub all around didn't burn. Not one bit.

She realized, then, that her body count had risen to two. Two more than she ever wanted. At that point, she lost track of what was going on as she let the phoenix take control. It dealt better with the life-and-death stuff—especially the death stuff—than her human side.

Before she knew what was happening, her phoenix form had launched little firebombs all around the area, targeting those who had fallen or tried to run away. Apparently, her phoenix half was a bloodthirsty and unforgiving creature. It was turning them all to ash. *She* was turning them all to ash.

She gave up trying to count the bodies. She was going to have to come to terms with the power of the phoenix and its unwillingness to let any evil person survive encountering it. She made a few more passes to be certain she got them all, but when the smoke cleared and the area was cleansed to her bird-side's satisfaction, Syd dropped down to the ground, landing in an ungraceful heap near Paul and Arthur.

She lay there, shivering in her feathers, unsure of what to do next. She was still a bird. How did she get back to her human shape? Would she ever walk on two feet again rather than fire-tipped claws and feathers? Panic made her shake as she watched Paul approach.

He crouched down next to her. "You did very well, *dragostea mea*. Thank you. Kreegar was a powerful mage. A powerful enemy. Alone, I don't know that I would have bested him, but you took him out like he was nothing. I'm so proud of you."

She opened her beak but refrained from vocalizing when she recalled what had happened when she screeched at Kreegar. She didn't want to hurt Paul. Never did she want to hurt Paul.

"Are you ready to come back to us?" Arthur's voice came from over Paul's shoulder. He shook out a Native weave blanket and placed it over her shivering form. She felt the goodness of him—the magic that was Arthur—envelop her immediately, and she felt safe. "You did very well for a first-timer, Sybil."

And just like that, she felt herself changing. She shifted into her human form to find that she was naked. Thank goodness Arthur had thought to bring her a blanket. Too much had happened in the past few minutes. Dealing with being naked in public—well, in front of two men—right now wasn't something she wanted to deal with. Even if one of the men was hunky Paul. Arthur was a father figure to her and that just screamed of wrongness to her human sensibilities.

"I'm sorry," she said, her voice raspy. "I kind of lost control at the end there and let the phoenix take control. I didn't go up there intending to...uh...kill them all."

"Sadly, when evil takes hold in a soul, there is usually no alternative," Arthur said in a contemplative tone. "All of the people who came here today were pledged to evil. They could not be allowed to continue on their path, and I doubt any of them could have been saved. They were following the orders of a blood path mage. Once someone has started down the blood path, there's no going back. All of these had that taint."

Paul's head rose as they all heard the roar of powerful engines in the distance. Motorcycles, Syd thought. It sounded like a bunch of them were coming up the winding drive to Arthur's home.

"Sounds like the cavalry has finally arrived. I'll go greet them," Paul said, rising to his feet. He helped Syd stand, as well, tucking the blanket around her briefly before turning her over to Arthur's care.

Syd went with Arthur when he coaxed her toward his house. She was bone tired but also a little exhilarated. She'd done something. Something good, despite the...um...killing...which she still had to figure out. She'd helped Arthur and Paul fight off the bad guys. She'd found her strength, despite not really understanding—or actually believing—she could be a mythical shapeshifter.

"You were glowing," she said absently to Arthur, remembering the sight of him, wearing a glowing translucent outfit of ancient style. He'd held a staff and his leather clothes were beaded and had long fringe. He'd looked magnificent.

"It is part of my calling. When the need is great, Mother Earth protects me with Her power. I am what some call a Knight of the Light, though that's the European term that's popular in this age. In old times, we were called other things." He shrugged. "The words do not matter. It is the heart that is steadfast and true that means all."

He had his hand under her arm, guiding her in a role reversal of what was usual with the disparity in their ages. Syd was shaky, and Arthur was strong as an ox and still emitting a warm glow of power that teased her senses with a comforting security that made her feel safer than she ever had before.

Paul intercepted the wolves. Stone had arrived with most of his Pack. Slade was with them.

"Your phoenix flew," Slade said, coming over and shaking Paul's hand.

"That she did," Paul answered proudly. "Saved our skins, too. The mage was a strong one. He made some interesting claims that I'd like to pass on to the leadership. Can you assist with that?"

"Absolutely. He was a talker?" Slade looked intrigued.

"A boaster who tried to get me to change sides. He claimed my kind is on their side in this, but I think he was talking out of his ass, as the Americans say." Paul walked with Slade back toward where Stone waited with his men. "First, let's deploy the troops, just in case she didn't get them all."

Slade agreed, and they stopped to talk over coverage strategy with Stone. The wolf Alpha stayed with his men when Slade and Paul went up to Arthur's house. Most of the Pack had shifted and taken to the rugged areas all around the perimeter. They were following scent trails and making sure no other surprises were lurking in the shadows. A few others were on cleanup detail, removing any remaining traces of the attackers. Stone had agreed to dispose of their vehicles, as well, including the rather fancy luxury number Kreegar had arrived in.

That taken care of, Paul's attention returned to thoughts

of Syd. Arthur had taken her inside, so Paul led Slade up to Arthur's door and knocked. The old man came to the door and looked hard at Slade, then said something that surprised Paul.

"Welcome, young brother." Arthur's magical regalia had faded, but there was still a tangible power about the old shaman that Paul respected.

Slade looked surprised. "I didn't know there was one such as you in these parts," Slade said to the older man as they entered.

"I am here for a reason, which I suspect will soon be fulfilled," Arthur answered cryptically.

Arthur led them to the small sitting room where he invited them to take seats on the old overstuffed furniture. Paul was feeling the pains of the battle just past, so he was glad to sit for a few minutes, knowing the wolves were guarding the perimeter.

Syd was nowhere in sight, but Paul sensed her presence not far away. He heard running water and realized she must be in bathroom, washing up. He had no doubt Arthur was taking good care of her. There was a bond of friendship between them that was obvious to see. It was strong—almost that of a parent and child, though of course, they were not related by blood. Still, there was that unique bond that joined them in magic…and love.

Arthur brought out tray with tall glasses and a pitcher of lemonade from the kitchen, and then, the three men sat down and discussed what had just happened. Paul told Slade what Kreegar had claimed, and Slade made mental notes for later report to the Lords of all were in this part of the world.

Syd returned in the middle of their talk. She was wearing a terrycloth robe Arthur had provided, and she took a seat on the sofa next to Paul. He liked that. She snuggled into his side without demur, and he liked that even more. He put his arm around her shoulders, needing the contact. He needed to feel the soft shape of her form, the solid reality of her, sitting next to him.

After all that had happened, he just needed to have her nearby.

"Syd, this is Slade. He is a holy man among shifters and an old friend," Paul told her, introducing them.

Syd nodded at Slade as she reached for a glass of lemonade. "I didn't know Paul had any friends in this part of the world," she said, though her voice was still a bit scratchy. "Nice to meet you."

"I only just arrived a short while ago. Paul and I first met far from these shores, years ago. We go back a ways. These days, I've been living near Las Vegas with my mate," Slade informed her in a friendly tone.

"Thank you for coming to help," Syd said politely.

"I would've had to come sooner or later, anyway. There's been a lot of magical activity here lately, and part of my job is to keep tabs on this sort of thing and report back to the Lords. They keep track of the bigger picture, and I'm one of their field agents."

"Among other things," Arthur put in with a wry chuckle that made Syd look a little confused, but neither Arthur nor Slade was elaborating.

"And then, there were three," Slade said after a pause, looking directly at Syd. "You are the third phoenix shifter to manifest in this area, in the past few weeks. Let me guess. You're an orphan?"

Syd cocked her head in surprise. "Yes," she answered, dragging the word out. "I was raised by foster parents, but we never really bonded," she explained. "Probably because I was a tough kid and didn't open up much to them."

"I bet you also sensed things about them that made you not trust," Slade said softly, drawing her out. Slowly, Syd nodded.

"I could always tell when someone was lying to me. Even when I was little," she admitted. "Did you just say there are two other phoenixes in the area?"

Slade nodded. "One was raised like you, in the foster care system. He was supposedly an orphan. The other had only her grandmother, and they now believe he is related to their family through a lost relative. You might be, as well, since the shifter genes had to come from somewhere."

"You're saying I might have family out there? Like, real blood relatives?" She sounded so shocked and, yes, hopeful that Paul really hoped it was true for her sake.

He knew what it was to get your hopes up about finding family. He'd just found some distant relatives in Grizzly Cove, and that meant more to him than he could express in words. He hoped Syd would find the same.

"I believe so," Slade said seriously, then smiled. "And you just admitted you'd know if I was lying." He winked at her, and she smiled.

"I want to meet them," she said immediately.

"But you need to stay here tonight," Arthur put in quickly and firmly. "I have a guest cabin out back. I want you both to stay here. The other phoenixes can come up here if you can't wait, but I suggest you take one night, at least, to recover. You're not going anywhere, right now. This is where you need to be."

Paul was surprised when Syd didn't argue with the old shaman. She merely nodded and got a spooky look in her eyes. "Yes. I feel that, though I don't know why."

"I do," Arthur told her with a sparkle in his old eyes. "Trust me."

It was decided rather quickly that all three phoenixes would gather at the car lot where Stone and company worked tomorrow night, after the work day was over. Syd had decided on the time, and while Paul was surprised that she would wait that long, he suspected she knew something, or sensed something about the future that made her choose it. He wasn't going to argue. Arthur was insistent on them staying up on the mountain with him at least overnight.

Paul had seen the old shack near the face of the mountain that Arthur referred to as a guest cabin from the air. It had looked sound, and Paul was just as glad not to have to make the trip down the mountain after the drawn-out battle. He was just tired. Bone weary. He'd used a lot of energy, and this place was both cleansed and easily defensible now that they had the wolves in play.

Stone had agreed to keep a watch on the mountain—a small band of wolves who would slink around in their fur, keeping an eye on things. At the first sign of trouble, the wolves would howl, sounding the warning. It was enough. Paul would be able to rest easier knowing that someone was watching over the perimeter.

Slade left when most of the wolves headed down the mountain, taking the vehicles of the *Venifucus* with them. He told Paul he was going to report back to the Lords on everything they'd learned today, and he also promised to share the new intel with the bears in Grizzly Cove. Paul would've called, but he was just too tired to do more than get himself and Syd settled in the guest cabin before sleep caught him.

That happened, sometimes, after a great expenditure of magical energy. Sleep would restore them both, but it would take a few hours. Syd was already asleep when Paul carried her into the cabin and placed her on the bed. He followed her down after a quick recon of their new quarters showed no threats, and that was all he knew for several hours.

When Syd woke, it was dark. At first, she didn't recognize where she was, but the fact that Paul's warm arm was around her middle made her feel safe. Memory returned as she blinked the sleep out of her eyes a few times. She felt groggy and sore in spots, especially around her shoulders and arms. She remembered flying with a sort of wondering smile and realized her arms were sore because she'd been using the feathered versions to fly around the mountain.

She supposed, in time, she'd build up her muscles so she wasn't so sore after every flight. Then, she marveled at that thought. She could freaking fly.

"Are you thinking of me?" Paul's drowsy voice sounded rough near her ear. "Is that why you're smiling?"

"I'm thinking about flying," she admitted, still too stunned by her own thoughts to offer a sarcastic response.

His arm tightened briefly around her midsection. "I will love to fly with you," he whispered, and she'd never heard anything sexier. "I don't have feathers, obviously, but I can still teach you a few things about aerodynamics, I think."

She turned in his arms to face him. "I'd like that." She reached upward slightly to kiss him. "I think I have a lot to learn, and a lot of muscles to build. My shoulders are really sore," she admitted, still smiling.

He moved one of his big, warm hands to her shoulder and started a gentle massage that made her want to melt into a puddle. He knew just where to touch to make her muscles begin to relax.

"Here," he said, lifting upward until he was sitting on the side of the bed. "Roll onto your stomach, and I'll give you a proper rub down."

She was too sore to argue, and after that little sample, she was convinced he could make her feel better if given half a chance. She turned onto her stomach, turning her head toward him so she could watch him.

Paul went into the small bathroom and emerged with a little plastic bottle in his hands. He approached the bed and opened the bottle, squirting a small amount of cinnamon-scented oil into his hands. He rubbed them together to warm the oil.

"I saw this earlier. Not sure why Arthur keeps his guest room stocked with bath oils, soaps and lotions, but the little closet in there is full of stuff. Not a lot of choice of scent, though. Most of it is cinnamon or spice," he told her, almost apologetically.

"That's okay. I love the smell of cinnamon," she told him.

"That's good," he replied, sitting on the side of the bed facing her. "I've been told that my dragon form and the smoke I produce when in that shape has a slight cinnamon flavor to it."

She nodded as best she could with her face laying on one

cheek. "It does. It's very pleasant. Not hellfire and brimstone at all," she told him, smiling wide.

"Your feathers have a more delicate scent," he told her in a low growl. "I'll have to think about the proper words to describe it. I'm no poet, but it's a spicy scent that reminds me of the Orient."

"Sounds mysterious," she told him sleepily as he began to rub the oil on his hands up, under the loose shirt Arthur had loaned her, over her bare skin in slow, sensual circles. It felt wonderful.

"Exotic," he told her, his voice dropping low. She felt the feather light touch of his lips on one shoulder. "And beautiful." He paused to kiss her other shoulder. "Just like you."

She held her breath, hoping he would take it further, but he returned to massaging her shoulders and back. She didn't resist when Paul pushed the shirt up over her head and off. In fact, she helped by lifting up enough to shimmy the fabric out from under her. As far as she was concerned, she wanted nothing between his hands and her body.

He reached for a bit more oil and continued his work until her spine was jelly and her protesting muscles were completely mollified. She couldn't issue a single complaint about anything—except maybe the fact that he wasn't inside her yet.

The massage had done more than soothe her soreness. It had brought about an aching awareness. A pulsating awareness that demanded satisfaction. A satisfaction that she knew, from previous experience, only Paul could give. She wanted him. Deeply. Madly. Passionately.

Rolling onto her back, she looked up into his eyes, gratified to see the fire simmering in the depths of his gaze. He wasn't as unaffected as she'd thought. Good.

She raised her hands to his shoulders as his hands worked their way around to her breasts, cupping her. The slickness of the oil was still on his fingers as he rubbed them over her nipples. It was a delicious sensation. One she would never forget. But she wanted more.

She coaxed his head down with gentle pressure on his neck until she could kiss him. The kiss deepened and seemed to wake the dragon within. She felt the fire of him blazing hot as he kissed her with a ferocity he must have held in check in their previous encounters.

She wanted it all, this time. She didn't want him to hold back. His magic rose and tickled hers—at least, that's what it felt like. She was new to her power, but she was starting to recognize its feel, its shape. His power seemed to tease hers, touching and gliding away, twining and untwining. It felt right, if a bit tentative, at first. The two types of fiery magic blended and separated, coexisting with harmony and a unique expression of each of their innate magics.

"Roll over," Paul growled when he finally released her from his masterful kiss.

She had an inkling of what he intended, and she was all for it. Going with the motion of his guiding hands, she rolled back onto her stomach, only to rise on her knees when he lifted her hips off the bed. He positioned her at an angle, her face on the soft pillow, her ass in the air, as he took his place behind her.

He didn't wait. He positioned himself and plunged into her. She was more than ready, skyrockets of pleasure going off behind her eyelids as he slid home in one long slide. Oh, that felt so good!

His thrusts pushed her upward, her chest rubbing against the soft fabric beneath her in the most delicious way. She moaned as he pulled out, drawing her back, then pushed forward again, restarting the process. Long, slow thrusts made her body sing with excitement, her nerves tingling in anticipation of his every move. Then, he started to move faster.

Altering his rhythm and moving at different angles, he kept her guessing and held her on the fine edge of rapture for a long, long time. He made her reach her limits and then pushed beyond, teaching her things about her body and its response to him—only him—and what she was truly capable of in the way of pleasure.

She screamed his name into the pillow as she came after long, drawn-out moments of being held back, on the precipice. When he finally let her tumble over, she went wholeheartedly, her body spasming around him, drawing him into her pleasure. She felt him stiffen and join her in ecstasy, a feeling of satisfaction filling her as she felt their magic join just as their bodies had, twining in rapture, then coming apart again, never again to be the same.

She was forever changed by what had passed between them. He'd introduced her, not only to her inner phoenix, but to a passionate side of herself that she hadn't quite realized existed. At least, not to this extent.

"You're amazing, *draga*," he whispered as he arranged them both on the bed, spent, fulfilled, and utterly drained. Even so, he'd made sure she was comfortable before collapsing next to her, and he spooned her, pulling her into his arms as he lay behind her.

He was the amazing one. "I've never felt...so much...before." She was still trying to catch her breath.

A masculine rumble of pleasure that wasn't completely human sounded from his chest. The phoenix inside her stretched in pleasure. It recognized the dragon in him as its equal...its...*mate?*

The word rang in her mind. It felt significant, but she didn't know enough about shifter culture to know exactly what that word entailed to them. To her, now that she was one of them. She would learn, in time, but until then, she'd be careful what she said aloud when words popped into her mind with a *knowing* that they were important.

"The sun will be up in an hour," Paul said sleepily from behind her. "Let us sleep until then, at least. When the sun rises, we have work to do."

She wasn't sure exactly what he meant, but she was sure there were things to be done. If nothing else, she wanted to check on Arthur and talk to him about everything that had happened. She had so much to learn.

But, first... She was going to enjoy being in Paul's arms, warm from his lovemaking. He truly was a special being, and for this moment out of time, he was all hers.

CHAPTER 12

Syd and Paul made their way over to Arthur's for breakfast. They had awakened shortly after dawn and spent a few soapy, sexy minutes in the bathroom, cleaning up and making love in the wide shower stall. Paul was an inventive lover with a sense of humor and play that kept her guessing and happy.

Although she would have liked to forget the real world and spend the rest of the day in bed with him, there were things to be done. They dressed and headed out to cross the distance to Arthur's home, stopping along the way to talk with Stone, who had walked up from the edge of the property, making himself visible. Syd hadn't seen him until he popped into view, and she jumped a bit. Werewolves, she was learning, were really good at being stealthy.

"Morning," Stone said to Syd. "Quiet night," he directed toward Paul.

"I'm glad. Thanks for your vigilance." Paul offered Stone a firm handshake of thanks, and Syd recognized the respect between the two men and the beginnings of a bond of trust that would only grow stronger as time passed and they worked together.

"The old man came out to talk to use at daybreak. He did some kind of sun welcoming ceremony. Even invited me and my Pack members to participate." Stone seemed impressed despite himself. "That's one special dude. Powerful and quieter than any holy person I've ever encountered before."

"Arthur is a gem," Syd agreed. "A kinder soul you will never meet."

"I asked him if he ever came down off the mountain. I think he'd be a good influence on some of my Pack, as well as the new phoenixes we seem to have acquired." Stone made a face that indicated his ongoing wonder at the emergence of such powerful beings in his area.

"What did he say?" Paul asked. Syd was curious, too. As far as she knew, Arthur hadn't been away from his home in years. Maybe decades. Perhaps even longer.

"He got kind of cryptic, but if I understood him correctly, he seemed to say that he couldn't leave just yet, but the time was soon coming when he would finally be free of his obligation and able to travel once more. He promised to stop by to meet Lance and visit with my Pack when he could."

Syd was impressed. "That's pretty amazing," she said aloud. "As long as I've known him, he's never even mentioned stepping foot off his property. I thought he was homebound."

Stone squinted and shook his head. "I don't think so, but he's got the inscrutable act down to T, so maybe I misunderstood."

Syd had to laugh. Stone had only just met Arthur the day before, but already, he had him pegged. "I think he enjoys being mysterious," she admitted.

"It's a shaman's prerogative, I guess," Stone agreed. "I'm heading down the mountain now, but there will be Pack members around all day, keeping watch. Arthur seems to think there won't be any more trouble, but by the same token, he thanked me for the continued perimeter guard."

"Which means he's *hoping* there's no further trouble, but he's not entirely certain there won't be," Paul interpreted.

"That was my take," Stone said, nodding. "Anyway, the day shift just arrived before you came out, and the night shift is heading down. I'll be back tonight. Call me if you need anything before."

Paul reached out and shook Stone's hand. "Thanks again, Alpha. You and your Pack have done me a great service here. I owe you one."

"Huh. That's pretty cool to have a dragon owe us a favor," Stone mused with a smile. "But don't worry. I won't ask you to burn Phoenix to the ground or anything."

They all had a good laugh, and Stone departed soon after, leaving Paul and Syd close to Arthur's door. They didn't even have to knock. Arthur must have seen them, and he greeted them at the door, welcoming them inside. Scents of scrambled eggs and bacon wafted through the air, and Paul's stomach rumbled loudly, making Syd giggle.

Arthur refused to discuss anything important until after they'd all eaten. He had cooked up a storm and laid his small table with more food than Syd had ever seen. Her stomach rumbled, and suddenly, she was ravenous. Hungrier than she could ever remember being before in her life.

"I thought you would have a delayed reaction," Arthur said when he saw Syd eyeing the food. "Every first timer I've known got really hungry after their first shift. I was surprised you didn't eat that much last night, but I guess weariness won out over hunger. Don't wait for me," he ordered her in a friendly tone as he pushed a plate in front of her. "You need to feed and feed well. Shifting takes a lot out of a person, and food is the best way to replace the energy you use when you shift."

"You mean I'll be able to eat more now that I can shapeshift?" Syd asked, realizing there were some pretty amazing benefits to her new abilities that she hadn't considered.

"Every shifter I've ever known could eat as much as they wanted and never had to worry about burning it off. The real problem is if you can't get enough food to fuel your increased metabolism. Shifters can waste away faster than humans if they don't have a steady supply of food."

"Well," Syd paused in the middle of filling her plate with

more than she'd ever eaten in one sitting, "it seems there are some hidden benefits to this shifting thing. I think I'm going to like not having to watch every calorie."

They shared breakfast and idle conversation, steering clear of any heavy topics at Arthur's direction. Once they were finished, Syd and Paul offered to clean up, and Arthur accepted their help gracefully. He went into the sitting room and waited for them there.

Syd was really curious about what Arthur might tell them, but she figured he'd give her more information on what she had become. Syd really didn't know how much Arthur knew, but it was probably a lot.

Still, the topic of conversation when they finally rejoined him in the sitting room shocked her. Arthur didn't waste words. He started right in with a direct query.

"What do you know of dragons?" He was asking Syd, much to her surprise.

"Not much. Just what you and Paul have told me and what little I've seen in visions," she admitted. "Why?"

"I have lived here for many years. Many more than you probably suspect," Arthur told them, not answering her question directly. "I have been fulfilling a promise I made long ago to beings of great power. I have been safeguarding their resting place in service to the Mother of All. It is my calling and my duty. Also, my great honor."

"Wait a minute." Paul seemed taken aback. "Are you saying, you're the guardian of a dragon's resting place?"

Arthur gave him a sly smile. "More than one, actually. Over a century ago, a group of your brethren decided to sleep until the world needed them again. They were led by a golden hunter who had some ability to see the future. He knew that the dragons would need to rise, in time, and if they did not protect themselves before that time, the enemies of all that is good would pick them off one by one. So many of your kind have been lost over the years, Paul." Arthur looked solemnly at Paul, compassion in his old eyes. "I am almost certain your parents were killed by the enemy, but somehow, they managed to hide you among the humans. That is why you have survived. That, and your own determination to follow the right path."

"I saw dragons underground and a golden dragon superimposed on a blond man," Syd said.

"You saw their resting place," Arthur confirmed. "I have been there a few times to check on them, but my duty is to guard the entrance to their hidden domain."

"It's here?" Paul asked, clearly excited by the idea.

"The entrance is hidden, but it is nearby. I will show it to you, as your arrival here, and the battle that just occurred, tell me the time for the last dragons to rise has arrived."

Syd clutched Paul's hand. This was amazing. She was so happy for him.

"The journey to reach the dragon's nest is not easy. They lie far, far below in a chamber few can access." Arthur told them as he got to his feet and led the way outside. "You need not bring anything with you except this." He handed Paul a coin. It looked like an ordinary piece of dull copper. Sort of like an oversized penny with no markings on it that Syd could see at first glance.

"Give that to the golden dragon. It will show him that you traveled to him with my blessing. The fact that you are a dragon counts in your favor, but the dragon folk sleeping below are wary of strangers with good reason. Remember that, and you should be fine." Arthur stepped out into the sunshine and walked them toward the old guest house where they had stayed the night before. It butted up against the side of the mountain in back, and it was there that Arthur pointed. "The old mine entrance is behind the guest house."

Syd and Paul followed Arthur into the small shack and to the back wall of the building. There was a built-in closet arrangement there that Arthur walked up to. He selected a particular door to the left of center, then pressed one of several coat hooks upward. A small click sounded, and the back of the closet popped as it swung back about two inches into darkness.

"A secret entrance," Syd breathed, totally impressed. This was like something out of a movie. A very cool movie.

Arthur led the way in, hitting a switch inside the secret passage that illuminated a string of bare lightbulbs leading down a narrow passageway, deep into the mountain.

"I've updated the place a few times over the years. We run off solar power now, for the most part," Arthur told them. "The sleepers come up and visit me every few years to see what's been happening in the world and binge on pop culture, so they don't get too far behind. They like to tinker with new tech, so they helped a lot with the upgrades. And, of course, they do all the work underground. I just source the parts and tell them where to get them. They do the pickup, bring the bits back and install them."

"So, they're not really sleeping at all, are they?" Syd asked as they walked down the well-lit and surprisingly clean passageway.

"Oh, no. They do sleep for long stretches of time. But they knew going in that they'd have to hit the ground running when they finally emerged, so they made provision to wake every decade or so in shifts, to keep current with developments in the world and check how the mortals were doing. When they wake, they stay in the guest house, which is why I keep it ready."

"When was the last time one of them was awake?" Syd asked, curious as they kept walking down the long and twisting passageway.

"At least four or five years ago now," Arthur replied as they came to the end of the passageway. It opened rather abruptly into a low-ceilinged area that held what looked to Syd like mining implements and other odds and ends. There was a work bench along one wall that had various bits and bobs, tools, parts, and spools of wire and what looked like fiber optic cabling.

"This is one of the workshops," Arthur explained as he led them past the piles of boxes and crates that held pieces of equipment and replacement parts. "Over here is what you'll need. The railway."

It didn't look like any kind of railway Syd had ever seen, except maybe in old documentaries about mines. A narrow rail system led downward into darkness and a set of carts that were badly dinged up and dented, though not too dusty, were sitting on a side rail, as if waiting to be used. Arthur walked up to one of them and opened the double doors, exposing the inside of the cart.

A light popped on as the door opened, displaying a surprisingly comfortable-looking interior. There were two seats—one on either end of the cart—that were well upholstered in dark leather. Hand rails were installed all around, probably because the ride was more roller coaster than railroad, if Syd had to guess. Windows were all around at what would be eye-level when seated. Arthur reached in and knocked on the strip of glass.

"Thick Plexiglas. Won't break if any rocks get kicked up. They try to keep the rail system as clean as possible, but it's only used every few years, and rocks will be rocks." Arthur shrugged and smiled.

"But what if part of the tunnel is collapsed or something? If nobody's been down here in four or five years, how do we know it's still safe?" Syd wanted to know. She was feeling a lot of trepidation about getting in this rolling chamber of horrors and plummeting down into who-knew-what.

"We upgrade everything all the time. If there had been a collapse, I'd know," he told her. "There are sensors placed throughout and they report back to my cell phone. I get immediate updates if something happens, and I have a way of contacting the dragons when needed so they can effect repairs. We haven't had to do that very often, but on two occasions in the past fifty years, I had to wake someone up to fix something. Otherwise, I can usually take care of things on my own."

"And, here, I thought you were a lonely shut-in, unable to fend for yourself," Syd chided, smiling at Arthur and touching his arm. "In reality, you've been like Alfred, the keeper of the superhero's cave, all these years." Arthur smiled as Syd chuckled.

"Just get in the car and press the button. Everything is automatic, and lighting will come on in each section as you go along. If it doesn't, don't worry. The downhill ride is mostly powered by gravity, anyway. It's only when you're coming back up that you might need the electric engine, but even then, there are no grades so steep that you couldn't get out and walk or crawl in some of the lower spots," Arthur assured her.

"Will everybody be asleep when we arrive?" Paul asked, already climbing into one of the seats, clearly eager to be on his way.

"Hans will probably wake before you get there. He sleeps closest to the entrance by design, and he'll likely hear you coming long before you arrive."

"He's the golden one," Syd reasoned, wondering if her vision would prove to be accurate.

Arthur nodded. "He is. And he is their leader. Talk to the golden dragon first, and all will be well. He'll recognize Paul right off, though I'm not sure what he'll make of you, Syd." Arthur winked at her, and she hoped he was just joking around.

She really didn't want to become a dragon snack so soon after finding her own power. At least she didn't have to fear the dragon's fire. She doubted anything could burn a phoenix. And, now, she had some powers of her own. She wasn't sure what she could do against a dragon, but she was certain Paul wouldn't let any of them threaten her. She trusted him to keep her safe with his unknown brethren.

Arthur slapped the side of the cart and stepped back as they boarded. Just before the door shut completely, Arthur caught her eye.

"Don't forget to look up when you can. It's a beautiful ride, if you watch for the wonders." With those last words, he stepped back, and Paul released the mechanism that had held the cart still. It began a slow roll that increased when Paul pushed another button on the center console.

She heard an electric hum that must be the engine whirring to life, taking them slowly, at first, toward the main line. Syd waved to Arthur who watched them leave. He waved back just as they rounded a bend, and within a moment, he was out of sight.

The noise wasn't as bad as Syd was expecting, though the cart did rumble over the rails and jostle her around on the padded seat. As Arthur had promised, lights came on in the next section of track as they approached, and she had a pretty good view out the small windows. Now that she was seated inside the cart, she saw that the top of it was also made of a much larger sheet of clear material. There wasn't much to see above, at the moment, because the tunnel they were in was narrow on all sides, including the ceiling, but she got her first glimpse of an enormous cavern as they crested the first small hump in the track and the engine cut out.

Gravity took them downward at an increasing pace as they entered a space where the ceiling—and the lights—were a good fifty yards up. This was no man-made chamber. The rock here had been forged by Mother Nature into wild patterns of red, gold, and brown. The striations were lovely, and they sped by at increasing speed as they trundled downward in the cart.

"Nice view," was Paul's comment as he looked out at the scenery.

They were back into a narrow part of the tunnel before she could reply.

"We seem to be going awfully fast," she said, watching the rock face speed by very close now to the windows. "Are you sure this is safe?"

"Do you trust your friend, Arthur?" was Paul's reply.

The thought calmed her. Arthur would never knowingly lead her astray. He had a good soul and a pure heart. If he put them on this path, she had to believe it would turn out okay.

Syd nodded just as another cavern lit up before them. The little cart came out of the tunnel into a place where the track curved around the side of a cliff, spiraling downward. There were lights along the walls, and though she couldn't see the top or bottom of the wide shaft they were circling, the walls glittered with golden ore.

"Looks like there's gold in them there hills," she muttered. The cart had slowed as it approached the curves, and it took them at a sedate pace.

"Smells like a very pure ore," Paul commented. "I suspect this old gold mine is the source of the dragons' wealth."

"Wealth?" Syd echoed, still fascinated by the sparkling walls rushing by.

"How else do you think they afford to keep upgrading this place. They sleep all the time. Nobody's working to earn a living down there. They must just take a little gold from this mountain when they need cash. They can fly somewhere where gold is plentiful, like the Yukon, and sell it for cash. I'm sure there's a way around the paperwork, or some human mining operation willing to aid them by mixing the dragon gold in with their own for a small percentage. Hard commodities like gold and gemstones are easy to convert to currency, if you know the right people—and there are always people around willing to help for a cut of the action."

When they'd gone around several wide loops of the spiral, the track led them back into a tunnel on a straight track that led downward at a sharper angle. The speed of the cart rose, again, and Syd kept her eyes on the path ahead. There was one dark spot where a light bulb had apparently burnt out, but thankfully, the rest of the string was functioning properly and their pathway deeper into the mountain was well lit.

Sometime later, they came out into the largest cavern yet. Their track hugged one side of the enormous chamber. There was a very large waterfall on the other, splashing down into a large lake far below then trickling away into an underground stream. Syd's breath caught at the sight.

"I bet they swim here," Paul said. "That lake looks big enough for a couple of dragons." The cart went around the outside of the enormous cavern, which allowed them time to take in the scenery. "Look, there's a parking area with a cart in it. I suspect they come up here for a swim or a drink of the water, then can go right back down to their nest," Paul said with some excitement in his voice. "Nice design."

"Yeah," Syd agreed. "All the comforts of home." She smiled as he did, sharing in the moment of wonder. Then, she saw another tunnel entrance coming up. "Looks like we're going back in."

Paul nodded as he followed the direction of her pointing finger to the tunnel. "I wonder what we'll see next."

This tunnel was longer than the others. Just when Syd was going to question the duration of the narrow passage, they emerged into a magical cavern that glittered with crystals. She recognized quartz, amethyst and topaz right away, but there were other, more precious crystals shining back at her. The walls were covered with natural formations—like the inside of a giant geode—but there was definitely a pile of raw and cut gems in one area. A big pile. Like, a *really* big pile.

"What were you saying about gold and gemstones?" she said to Paul, sending him a sideways glance.

"This is probably part of their treasury. A place to deposit hard commodities, safer than any bank." He smiled as his own observation and she couldn't help but grin. There was something incredibly special about not only their location, but the man she was sharing this fairytale journey with. Paul was *her* treasure.

They exited the crystal cavern into another tunnel, this one longer and more winding than the others. The cart slowed again as it rounded sharp turns, but they kept going downward until...

The cart emerged into a massive cavern. Unlike the rest of their path, the lights didn't come on to illuminate the entire place. Only one light fixture lit the landing platform where a few other carts were parked. It was a chandelier. Made of pure gold.

It was ornate. Like something out of another age. A master work of a goldsmith from another time and place that had been retrofitted with discrete electric bulbs. What little Syd could see of the walls of the cavern were gleaming, polished gold.

"I think we just found where all the gold is," Paul whispered, his words echoing slightly in the large space.

"This is what I saw," she told him. "Not the chandelier or the walls, but the landing and the depth of the cavern. The dragons are sleeping over there." She stretched out her arm, and a large golden dragon's head loomed out of the darkness beyond the ring of light from the chandelier.

Syd pulled back, jumping despite herself. Paul pushed forward, stepping in front of her as if to shield her from the dragon.

"Why have you disturbed our sleep?" the dragon hissed in as quiet a tone as a giant reptile could manage.

"I've been looking for you all of my life," Paul said, his voice low and filled with emotion. Syd's heart went out to him.

"What is your name, young one?" The golden dragon looked intrigued.

"I am Paul Lebchenko, and I was raised an orphan. I've been looking for other dragons since I first shifted, and you are the first I have found."

A tear slid down Syd's cheek on Paul's behalf. This was such an important moment for the man she loved.

Yes, loved. She had come to realize it, at some point, but hadn't really admitted it to herself. It was all still so new, but she loved him. With all her heart.

Between one eye blink and the next, the golden dragon morphed into a man. He had golden hair and was dressed in clean denim as he walked out of the darkness and into the circle of light. He was the man she'd seen superimposed on the dragon in her vision.

"Lebchenko," he repeated as if considering the name. "I knew a dragon of that name centuries ago. He would not heed the warnings and seek safety, because his mate was human and afraid of the world down below. You could be his

143

son."

"I might be. Frankly, I have no idea how I came to be in the orphanage. Only that they had my name and a baby blanket that I keep locked away with my treasures," Paul admitted.

The golden man smiled. "All dragons lock away their treasures," he agreed. "Perhaps, one day, I can examine this blanket to see if it holds any trace of my long-ago friend."

"I'd like that," Paul agreed.

"But who is this you bring to us?" the dragon asked, making a gesture toward Syd, who was still placed strategically behind Paul.

"She is mine," Paul announced clearly.

"A woman of power," the golden dragon said in a questioning tone.

"Syd?" Paul turned slightly toward her, not giving his back to the strange dragon but inviting her to join in the conversation. She stepped forward, to stand next to Paul.

"I'm Syd," she said to the dragon-man. "I saw this place in a vision," she told him, looking around beyond the circle of light cast by the chandelier toward where she knew the other dragons lay sleeping.

"Syd? It is a strange name for a female," was the dragon's comment.

Syd sighed. "It's short for Sybil. I don't like that name."

The man laughed. "It is more than your name. It is what you are, if you have visions. You are a Sybil. A foreseer. Are you not?"

"I guess," she hedged. "It only started recently, and I'm not all that comfortable with it yet."

The man chuckled and moved closer. "I am Hans Gilder." He reached out to shake Paul's hand, and even Syd felt the clash of power as the two men gripped each other's hands. Their magic met and evaluated each other, then receded like a tide.

Hans turned to her, and she gave him her hand, but he didn't shake. Instead, he lifted her hand to his lips and placed a kiss on the back like something out of an historical novel. Yeah, if she hadn't met Paul first, this guy would've looked like some kind of Prince Charming. As it was, her heart had already been claimed by a dark-haired prince of a guy who had saved her life over and over. She could not be swayed by golden good looks.

"Ah." Hans stepped back, away from her. "But you are more than a Sybil. You are a woman of greater power."

"She is a phoenix," Paul said boldly, declaring the magic Syd was still a bit uncomfortable with. Hans's eyes narrowed.

"A phoenix? Is she the only one?" he asked abruptly.

"She is the last of three to emerge in recent weeks in the nearby city."

Hans looked crestfallen. "Then, the time has come at last." His gaze lowered, for a moment, and he breathed a deep sigh. "When the phoenixes rise and do not cycle back to the sun, it means they are needed. And, if they are needed, then so are we."

CHAPTER 13

"It's just like my vision," Syd whispered to Paul as dragon heads on long, scaled necks started rising all over the giant golden cavern.

Hans had hit the switch to begin illuminating the far reaches of the massive cavern, and one by one, the sleepers had begun to wake. After a lot of yawning, stretching and then shapeshifting into their human forms, a dozen or more dragons had gathered around their leader, eyeing the newcomers curiously.

Hans didn't waste time. He introduced Paul as a fellow dragon but didn't leave time for questions. He gave orders to his brethren to gather the things they might need in the outside world and begin making their way upward. Apparently, they'd laid out a detailed plan for when they woke, and there was a strategic deployment of modified mine carts with each dragon having a specific task to complete and a place in the rotation upward toward the surface.

Hans sent Paul and Syd ahead, back the way they had come in the very same mine cart they had taken down. He gave them instructions for Arthur only after Paul had produced the coin Arthur had given him. When Hans touched it, his magic had revealed that it was pure gold under the dull copper camouflage. It had a dragon's head imprinted in gold. Hans's profile, if Paul wasn't much mistaken.

Paul wanted to talk to the other dragons, but he'd been given his marching orders. They had work to do, and he and Syd were only in the way at the moment. He knew his best bet was to follow instruction and go back to the surface with Syd, but it was hard to leave the dragons' nest behind when he'd only just found them.

Syd put her hand in his. "We'll see them again on the surface," she said in a soft voice as Hans turned away, already working with his people. Paul and Syd had been dismissed, it seemed.

"I know..." Paul didn't want to say anything where the dragons might hear. He didn't want them thinking he was pathetic. "Thank you for being here with me," he told her instead, reaching down to give her a kiss.

"Always, Paul," she whispered against his lips. "I'll always be there for you. I promise."

Now, that sounded serious, and just what his dragon needed to hear. The anxious part of him settled. Who needed anyone else when Syd was here, with him?

With a last look at the magnificent cavern he might never see again, Paul ushered Syd back into the mine cart and pushed the button that would take them back.

On the surface of the mountain once again, Paul and Syd found Arthur waiting for them. They'd been gone for hours, and morning light had faded to mid-afternoon. Arthur invited them to his place for a late lunch. He'd been busy while they'd been traveling who knew how many miles underground. He'd filled the guest cabin with things the returning dragons might need, from modern clothing to shoes and boots. The side walls of the old cabin had been opened up to reveal hidden compartments, like open lockers, each with someone's name on the front and belongings within hanging from hooks or stored in duffel bags.

Paul got only a quick glance at the transformation of the old building on his way out as Arthur ushered them through.

He led them straight to his own home, a few yards distant, and Stone joined them along the way. Paul nodded a greeting to the werewolf Alpha and received a concerned nod in return.

"I have some news," Stone told Paul in a low voice as he dropped back to walk beside Paul while Arthur went ahead with Syd. "Your lady's been outed in a big way. Bad guys are watching her home and place of work."

"Damn. I was hoping we could avoid that sort of attention, but too much has happened," Paul said as they neared Arthur's house. Syd and Arthur were waiting by the door for them to catch up, and Arthur invited Stone to join them inside.

All four went indoors to find the kitchen table piled high with sandwiches. Arthur had, indeed, been busy. After being instructed to help themselves, they each grabbed a sandwich from the huge pile and joined Arthur in the front room where they all could sit comfortably.

"Alpha," Arthur surprised Paul by starting the conversation by talking to Stone first, "you will have to tell your people. The dragons are rising. This part of the world is about to see a vast increase in magic, and your friends and family need to be aware of it."

"Dragons? Plural?" Stone asked, clearly surprised.

Paul nodded. "There is a nest of dragons waking under a distant mountain. We saw them. They're on their way to the surface. Their leader said the rising of three phoenixes was a sign that it was time for them to return to the lands of men, as well. Things are about to get really interesting, I think."

"Will you be able to keep that meeting with Lance?" Stone asked, looking from Paul to Syd and back again.

"It is more important now than ever," Arthur put in before Paul could answer. "You must keep your appointment with the phoenix if you are to learn to work together. You, Paul and Syd, are the pivot points. You are the two who will be the interface between phoenix and dragon. You both need to keep good lines of communication open with both groups."

"I won't argue with that," Syd said with a smile for the old shaman. "Arthur has never steered me wrong yet."

"It's getting late, though," Paul noted. "If we're going to make that meeting, we should probably fly down there."

"Won't people see us?" Syd asked, concern on her beautiful face.

Paul shook his head. "We're magical beings, *draga*. If we wish not to be seen, we will not be seen."

She looked skeptical but nodded. "If you say so."

Stone gave them detailed instructions on how to find the meeting place. It was out behind the car lot where there was a collection of houses spread out over the desert. Stone called ahead and asked Lance to fly up to meet them, and within the hour, a dragon and two phoenixes were circling the sky above the desert, in preparation for landing.

Paul was concerned. He wanted so much to protect Syd until she was steadier on her magical *feet*, so to speak, but he knew he had to let her fly free. Her inner nature was that of a firebird. She could not be contained. Trying to keep her in a safe little box would only smother her flame, and he could not bring himself to do that. No matter how much he worried for her safety in the harsh world in which they lived.

Stone's report about her workplace and home being watched had not come as a shock to him, though he supposed she would be upset when he finally broke the news to her. He was looking for a way to do it gently. To tell her she could no longer live in the home she had made for herself. He knew it would be a devastating blow, but he would be there for her. He would do his best to soften the pain.

With his love.

All that had happened had only proved to him beyond the shadow of doubt that she was his mate. He was deeply, truly, forever in love with her. He was just unsure how to tell her— and uncertain of her feelings. He knew she was his, but did she understand the reverse must also be true?

She was so new to all of this. She had only just learned magic truly existed. Flying was something she'd done only twice now, but the fact that she found it instinctive gave him hope. He had no idea if her instincts about mating had kicked in, as well? He would have to find out the hard way...when he laid his heart bare before her. Something he planned to do later this very evening, if events progressed as he expected.

He reasoned that her home would be safe enough for one last night. He'd help her pack whatever she wanted to save and then hire a shifter moving service to be certain her belongings were not tampered with or waylaid on their journey. They'd have to go into storage for a while, during which time Paul hoped to convince her to set up house with him. They'd find a place to settle, and then, after suitable time had passed, he'd make certain that her belongings reached them in clean—un-magicked—condition.

As of right now, he had no idea where they would go, but he knew in his heart that, wherever Syd was, that would be his home. He might have to talk her around to the idea, but he could be patient...and cunning, if need be. He'd win her heart, no matter how long it took, because he knew his own heart could not go on beating without her.

She wouldn't let that happen. She'd be there for him. He felt it in his soul.

Paul dropped to the ground first, landing smoothly before her so that, if she tumbled, he could catch her. Syd was so new to flying, he had to watch her landings so she didn't get hurt. Proficiency with take-offs and landings would come in time, and he already saw ways that he could help her learn, but for now, the best use of his presence was as a backstop...or perhaps a catcher's net.

Paul spread his wings wide to give her a target. He would catch her and wrap her in his wings—in his arms—and prove to her over and over how much he loved her.

Syd didn't quite bowl him over when she crashed into him, but she definitely needed to work on her landings. He caught her, regardless, and set her back on her feet as gently as he could. Her fiery feathers tickled against his dragon hide, showing him once again, that they were a perfect match for each other. The both burned hot, and neither could be harmed by the other's fire.

Flying with her by his side from Arthur's mountain to this desert area on the other side of the sprawling city of Phoenix had been truly life changing. He'd never flown with anyone before. Birds had been afraid of him, sensing the predator within. He'd had to avoid airplanes in case someone aboard was able to see through his magical shielding.

All of his flying had been done alone. As most of his life had been spent alone. He'd searched for family—for acceptance—for so long. To finally find it so easily seemed almost impossible. He'd only just recently discovered Peter and his *babushka* in Grizzly Cove. Their welcome had touched Paul's fractured heart deeply.

Now, to find not only his perfect mate, but that she was someone he could share the skies with… It was all just too much. He dared not blink, lest it disappear in a puff of magic.

Paul's wandering thoughts were brought back to Earth by the none-too-graceful landing of the other phoenix. The male. Lance. The owner of the car lot.

It was obvious to Paul that Lance hadn't been flying long either. His landing, while much better than Syd's attempt, had been a little wobbly. Paul had to give the man points for trying, though. It wasn't easy to learn the nuances of the air currents when you were new to flying. It had taken Paul years to perfect his style, and he still got turned ass-over-tea-kettle sometimes when the winds decided to play with him.

Sensing others in the area, Paul shifted shape back to his human form. He'd carried a small bag of clothing for Syd with him into the shift, and it came through intact. He opened the bag and held out a long tunic-style dress Arthur had provided from the stockpile of clothes he kept in the cabin for the dragons down below.

Syd walked around Paul until he was between her and the

other male. She was using Paul as a human screen, but he didn't mind in the least. Neither of the phoenixes had been raised as shifters to be comfortable with nudity when they came out of a shift. Paul was lucky, in that respect. For some reason, the dragon magic allowed him to take his clothes with him into the shift, so he'd never intentionally returned from his dragon shape naked.

Oh, there had been a couple of notable occasions when he'd first been learning about his other side when he'd made mistakes, but since gaining mastery over his shifting, he'd had a lot better control. He was glad of that now. He would help his mate learn and grow into her powers, and he'd be there for her whenever she needed him. Even if it was only to shield her from view.

Syd shifted quickly this time. The more she did it, the better she seemed to get at it. She slid the tunic dress over her head quickly and was presentable for human sensibilities in less than a minute. The male phoenix didn't have as easy a time of it. He stayed in phoenix form, sort of walk-hopping toward the house in the distance. Paul heard a motor start up, and within a few minutes, a four-wheel drive vehicle approached. He could feel the magic in the two women were in the car. The one driving felt like a mage, but the woman in the passenger seat felt like...fire. Fire shifter. She was the second phoenix. Had to be.

The Jeep pulled close to the male phoenix, and the woman who had been driving hopped out. She waved, shouting "Sorry! We're still new to all this," as she got a bag from the back of the vehicle and opened it, tossing a pair of jeans to the male phoenix.

Lance had worked his way over to the Jeep, and in a shimmer of fiery magic, he shifted, catching the clothing from the friendly woman who had to be his mate. The female phoenix in human form had also gotten out of the vehicle and started walking slowly toward Syd. In moments, Lance and his mate had caught up with the other woman, and the three approached Syd and Paul together.

The two sides stood there, facing each other in silence until the mage-woman broke it. "Hi," she said in a bright, cheery voice. "I'm Tina." She reached out to shake hands with Syd first, and Syd reflexively took the other woman's hand.

Raised human, Syd didn't yet know not to reach out to touch Others until you were certain of them. Paul had been raised human, as well, but he'd been neglected as a child, and it wasn't his custom to reach out to anyone, so he hadn't had to change his behavior once he became aware of the unseen world of magic and shifters.

"I'm Syd," she replied as the two women shook hands. Paul held his breath, but there was no attack, no flare of magic. The handshake was just that—a greeting. "And this is Paul," Syd went on, oblivious to his thoughts.

Paul reached out to take the other woman's hand when offered, knowing it was the polite thing to do. He also had an ulterior motive. Touching the woman's hand allowed him to get a taste of her magic—and she, his. Their hands met and held for a brief moment, but that was enough for Paul to make a judgment. Tina was okay. No taint of blood magic or evil about her.

"This is my husband, Lance," Tina said, introducing the male phoenix who stood beside her. "And this is his cousin, Diana."

The male and female phoenixes didn't reach out for a handshake. Lance was holding his breath, his expression tight, and Diana had tears gathering behind her eyes, even though she was smiling. It was Diana that spoke first.

"I think you're probably my cousin, too," she told Syd, one of the tears escaping to roll down her cheek, though she ignored it.

"I was raised in foster care," Syd replied, her voice hiding her emotion, but Paul knew she was wound tight on the inside. He put a hand on her back, offering silent support.

"I was, too," Lance finally spoke. "Never found my folks, but when I met Diana and her grandmother, they were finally able to fill in the blanks for me." Lance moved a step closer, hesitantly. "It's just possible that you're my little sister."

"How?" Syd croaked, her strangled voice filled with emotion. Paul stayed close. This was perhaps one of the most important moments of her life and he felt privileged to be here to see it.

"My grandmother—I call her Oma because she was born in Holland—had two children. My mother and a son, named Gustav. Uncle Gustav died before I was born, but he traveled to Phoenix a lot. We now believe he was involved with a human woman here, and for whatever reason, he didn't tell Oma. She didn't know he'd had a child—children—with anyone, so discovering Lance's existence was a miracle."

"For all of us," Lance put in, reaching out to put one hand on his cousin's shoulder. "I gave up on ever finding out where I came from, but when the phoenix started to emerge, I figured my origins had to be magical in some way."

"The phoenix gift runs in our family. It skips generations, at times, but it manifests on occasion—usually resulting in someone dying much too young as they shift for the first time and head straight for the sun, never to return," Diana added.

"That's so sad," Syd said, as if unsure what else to say. "How can you know that I'm related to you?"

"Well, you're a phoenix, for one thing," Diana said, chuckling slightly.

"And, in my earliest memories, I remember a little sister," Lance added, shocking them all, judging by everyone's expressions. "I always thought she must've been another foster kid and that I misunderstood, but it makes sense now, seeing you. I remember being really little, and there being a baby girl. I was disappointed you weren't a boy, but then, I remember being told I could help protect you and that I was going to be a good big brother." Lance paused and shook his head. "I suppose that was our father telling me that, but I don't remember his face, only the pep talk. I was maybe two or three years old. Too young to have solid memories, I guess."

Paul felt his heart racing for Syd. He knew what it meant to be alone in the world with no blood relations. She'd been as isolated as he had, in her own way. The gift she had for knowing when people were telling lies had kept her from forming any real bonds with anybody—except maybe Arthur. Paul's own isolation was more brutal, at the hands of a totalitarian regime that didn't give any real care at all to a nation's orphans. He'd survived, but only just barely, and he knew many of the children he'd grown up with had permanent scars both mental and sometimes physical from the way they'd been raised.

He'd never stopped hoping, though. He suspected Syd hadn't stopped dreaming of finding a family she'd never known either. And, now…here it was. She had a brother. And a cousin. And, from the sound of it, a grandmother.

Paul's heart leapt for her. He'd found kin of a kind when he'd discovered the other dragons. That was enough for him. At least for now. But this… This was something different and altogether special. He felt joy in his heart that his mate had discovered this truly amazing gift. The gift of family.

Syd couldn't really believe what Lance was saying. He was her brother? How in the world did that work?

Yet, she felt something toward him. Not like the attraction she felt for Paul, but something older, and more familial. She'd never really experienced such a feeling before. She hadn't really dared to dream she'd ever find people of her own to love and trust and be family, but she could tell that every word Lance and the newcomers had spoken was the absolute truth as they knew it.

He remembered a baby sister. He believed she was that baby sister from his earliest memories.

When he'd met them in the sky above this stretch of desert, she'd felt instant recognition. At the time, she'd put it up to her newly discovered phoenix side recognizing a creature just like itself, but perhaps, it had been more. What if that jolt of happiness had been the phoenix recognizing its sibling?

"This is new to me, too, Syd," Lance said quietly, his gaze holding hers and his words ringing with truth to her ears. "I grew up knowing I was an orphan. I know what it's like for you. But I also know now, what it is to have family ties, and I hope you'll allow us—me and Diana and Oma—to share that with you, too." He stepped closer and held out his arms. "I'm sorry I wasn't there for you like our father wanted, but I'm here now, and I'd like to get to know my baby sister."

That was it. Syd sobbed as she practically threw herself into Lance's arms. She hugged him tight. So tight. He was real. He believed they were siblings, and he wanted to get to know her. That was more than she ever could have dreamed would happen when she woke up this morning.

So much had happened in such a short time. She'd learned about magic and discovered the love of her life—though Paul didn't know it yet. She'd fought with evil people and learned of her own power. And now, she'd found people who claimed her as their own.

It was all a little surreal.

CHAPTER 14

After much hugging, they were all invited back to Lance's house, which was just a short walk away. Stone had come in about halfway through the evening spent at Lance and Tina's to report that all was well on the mountain, and activity had ratcheted up a whole lot. Arthur had suggested that the Pack could cease their patrols now that some of the dragons were back on the surface, and Stone had pulled his people back.

He'd stayed and sat with Diana, who turned out to be his mate. Syd had enjoyed seeing the couples together and learning a bit of their stories, even as she shared some of her own with them. They were good people who deserved happiness, and she was so glad they'd found love and become *mated*, as the shifters called it.

It would take time to really get to know them, but that was okay. Syd was already looking forward to meeting the woman they all called Oma, who was her grandmother, too. They were planning a get-together as soon as Oma returned from her trip to Europe. Apparently, when Diana had come into her power, a bit of it had spread back to her grandmother, who had a new lease on life. While the energy lasted, she had gone to see her childhood home in the Netherlands and had refused the offer of company.

Oma had said—according to Diana—that she wanted her

granddaughter to have a true honeymoon with her new mate and had used that as an excuse to go traveling as she hadn't been able to travel in decades. She checked in with the family back in Phoenix every few days and had reported that she was bringing back surprises for them all. She also hinted at renewing old contacts but wouldn't elaborate. Still, the feeling among those left behind was that Oma was on some kind of secret mission that only she fully understood. That was said half-joking and half-serious, which made Syd wonder what the old lady was up to.

At length, the conversation turned to dragons, and Paul was asked a lot of questions to which he didn't yet know the answers. Syd felt for him. He had been a lone wolf—make that a lone *dragon*—for so long, he didn't know the things they were asking him about. Everything he knew about being a dragon had been learned from trial and error, and Syd knew Paul was a bit uncomfortable with all the questions.

He hadn't really had time to talk with the other dragons yet. Not in any depth. Hans had gotten all commander-ish and sent everybody scurrying before Paul could ask any real questions. Syd hoped the golden dragon would slow down for a few minutes once everybody was aboveground and give Paul a chance to ask what he wanted to know.

"I'm not sure what Hans has in mind," Paul told them all. "He seemed to indicate that the rising of you three was the sign they'd been waiting for to wake up and rejoin the rest of us above ground."

"I never thought I'd ever see a dragon in my lifetime, much less fly alongside one," Lance said, his eyes filled with wonder. "You're really good at landing, too," he added. "I wonder if you could give us some pointers."

Paul chuckled. "I'd be glad to. It wasn't easy when I first started shifting. I crashed a lot in the beginning."

Lance and Diana were both nodding. "Same here," Diana replied. "Any advice you could give us would be greatly appreciated."

"I think maybe you're going to have to give us some flying

lessons, Paul," Syd said, smiling as she clutched at his arm, moving closer as they sat side by side around the big kitchen table with the others. "If you don't mind."

"Mind?" Paul took the opportunity to put his arm around her shoulders and give her a little hug. He was like a starving man, unable to touch her the way he wanted because they were in public. The hug helped, even if it was sideways and not front to front. He'd get her alone soon, and then, they'd be able to snuggle. "I was already planning to help Syd," he told the others, trying to push down his urge to be alone with her and speak civilly to the others. "Might as well make it a group thing if you're all interested. I'm sure you can share what you've learned about flying with feathers with Syd. I'm not sure how much will carry over from my kind of wings to yours, but I can definitely help with the take offs and landings. Those are pretty much the same, I think."

"That would be awesome," Diana said, relief in her tone as she smiled. Stone had put his arm around her shoulders, as well, and Lance was edging closer to Tina. Dinner had been prepared and consumed hours ago, and the night was beginning to wind down, as was the conversation.

There was still so much more to say, but it had been a very long day filled with all sorts of new things. Paul knew they all needed some time to think about everything that had happened and sort through the events, feelings and new knowledge that had been gained. More questions would arise, but there would be other days to talk and learn more about each other, thankfully. Now that they had found each other, Paul doubted they would ever lose touch.

It had been a good day. Now, he intended to finish it with an even better night.

"Do you think Syd's house is safe enough for tonight?" Paul asked Stone point blank as the conversation hit a lull.

"We've kept a standing watch. Nobody has infiltrated, though the place is definitely under some sort of observation. Nothing much, just a guy in a car, but it's still being watched.

I hate to say this, Syd, but you're probably going to have to move." Stone put into words the topic Paul had found hard to raise with her. Good. At least it was out in the open now.

Syd looked stunned. "I hadn't thought much about it, but I suppose you're right," she said slowly. "But where would I go?"

Paul tightened his arm around her shoulders and squeezed lightly. "You always have a place with me," he told her. They were dancing very close to things he wanted to talk about with her in private, but at least he could say that much.

She looked over at him and smiled. "There's time to figure it out," she said, making him wonder what was going on behind those gorgeous, mysterious eyes of hers. "But I'm too tired to think about it tonight. Too much has happened. All I want is a quiet night in my house, and then, we'll deal with the rest of it in the morning."

"If that's what you desire, then that is what you shall have," Paul promised her.

"I just want you to know," Lance put in quietly. "You're always welcome here."

She reached across the table to take her brother's hand and smiled at him. "Thank you for saying that, but I don't want to bring trouble to your door."

"We've already had trouble here. The *Venifucus* know about Lance, and they know to steer clear," Stone said in support of his cousin-in-law, friend and boss.

"Like I said, I can't think about it tonight. My brain is full." Syd laughed as she rose from the table. "Thank you for welcoming me into your home. I would like to return the favor once I figure out where I'm going to end up." She grinned, and they returned her smile. Syd's mood was light, even though she'd been made aware of the reality that she'd have to move. Paul was glad she was taking it so well.

Paul stood with Stone and Tina while Syd hugged first Diana, then Lance for a long time. Paul didn't mind waiting. He'd give anything to be close to his own family, just once, but he didn't begrudge Syd this moment of happiness and peace in her soul. He wanted everything good for her. For always.

At length, they said their goodbyes, and Paul and Syd drove off in a car Stone had arranged to loan them from the car lot. It's wasn't anything flashy. In fact, it was about as nondescript as a luxury car could get, and it had a purring engine under the hood that could handle just about anything in a chase other than a true racing car.

Paul approached Syd's house from a side street, pulled over a few blocks away, and called the number Stone had provided. It was the cell number of one of Stone's Pack members who was watching Syd's house. They would run off the other surveillance long enough for Paul to pull the car into Syd's garage and get them both inside the house.

Paul would reinforce his wards and then take his lady to bed. They wouldn't need much light. Not for what he intended. Just the two of them, a soft bed, and the rest of the night, during which he'd prove his love to her as many times as she'd let him.

It felt weird to be entering her home again after all that had happened. The house was the same, but everything else in her life had changed. Radically.

Most important of all, was the man who walked beside her. Paul went ahead to check the house and do some magic mumbo jumbo that he'd tried to explain a bit in the car, before she'd waved him off. She was overloaded with information and couldn't absorb any more, right now. She was very interested to learn about magic, but it would have to wait until her head was clearer. A good night's sleep in her own bed ought to help.

Of course, she planned to have Paul in her bed, too, so she wasn't sure exactly how much actual *sleeping* would occur. That was okay, though. Being with him calmed her and helped ground her. He was her anchor in the storm, her touchstone.

She didn't turn on any lights as she went through the

house. She had a few lamps on timers scattered around the house, and they provided enough illumination to get around, without revealing to anyone outside that she was back. She knew she couldn't stay in the house. It just wasn't a safe enough location. *Indefensible* was the word Paul had used.

She knew she'd have to move to a better location, but for just one more night, she would enjoy the little nest she'd built for herself in this place. Honestly, she didn't want to live here, anymore, anyway. Not after those evil bastards had invaded her home and tried to bug it. Not after she'd been bashed over the head here. No, she knew it wasn't safe. That fact had been clearly demonstrated already.

Nostalgia, though, was a tough thing to silence. She'd loved decorating this place and setting it up to her exact specifications. She'd lived here for a number of years, but she wasn't so attached to the place that she couldn't take her belongings and go elsewhere. At this point, she knew that, anywhere Paul was, that could easily become her home. If he was agreeable, of course.

She wished she knew, for sure, whether or not he was thinking about their relationship becoming permanent. She knew what she wanted. She wanted him. Forever. But what was on his mind? That, she'd have to discover. The sooner the better. But she didn't want to just blatantly ask and put him on the spot. Ultimatums were never a good tactic.

"The house is secure for the night," Paul reported when he found her in the bedroom, slipping off her shoes. "I've talked with the wolves watching the place, and the other watchers haven't come back yet, but they'll keep an eye out. In fact, they've doubled the wolf presence. There are a few extra canines in your backyard tonight, and they'll start howling if anything threatens the house." Paul came up to her and put his arms around her in a loose embrace. "Seems your family is making sure you're looked after."

She rested her head against his chest for a moment. "It still seems kind of unreal. This whole situation is going to take some getting used to."

He rubbed her back with soothing hands. "It'll be all right. You've passed every trial that came your way and are still fighting strong. I have faith in you."

She pulled back a bit, so she could look up at him. "I couldn't have done any of it without you, Paul. When bad guys invaded my home, you were the one who stopped them and made sure I was okay. When the visions confused the heck out of me, you showed up and helped me figure it out. And, when the sun pulled at me, I didn't follow its call...because of you. Because I wanted to be with you more than I wanted to follow the sun over the edge of the world. I still want that," she told him in a hushed whisper.

"Good," he rumbled back at her. "I want that, too."

He kissed her, and then, it was all heat and passion and clothes in the way. She pushed at his shirt while he stripped the tunic dress off her in one delicious slide of fabric against skin. She had to take her hands off him while the dress came off, but as soon as it was gone, she went right back to him, unable to keep away.

She stood, naked and vulnerable in his embrace, but she didn't really feel vulnerable. Not physically. Emotionally was another matter.

His shirt came off and was tossed across the room, and he paused. "You mean the world to me, Syd," he told her, his tone as serious as she'd ever heard it. Her breath caught.

"You mean the world to me, too," she replied in a hushed tone. "And more."

"Did you understand what Stone was saying about mating among shifters?" His gaze was intent. "That shifters mate for life?"

"It sounded so beautiful," she agreed as she nodded slowly. "And it felt right."

"It feels right to me, too," he told her. "Syd, I believe you are my mate. You're mine."

Her heart leapt in her chest, joy filling her at his words. "You're mine, too," she replied, unable to keep the teary smile off her face. She reached up and wrapped her arms around his shoulders, pressing close. Daring greatly, she whispered, "I want to keep you forever."

Paul kissed her then, a passionate kiss that spoke of love and possession, tenderness and joy. When he finally let her up for air, he met her gaze, and she could see the emotion in his dark eyes.

"I love you, *dragostea mea*, my heart. I will love you forever and beyond. We were meant to be together, and my heart is so happy that I've found you, it could burst." He placed tender kisses along her jaw as she giggled with happiness.

"Don't let that happen," she chided. "I feel the same, and I want to spend a good long time—the rest of our lives—with you."

He paused to meet her gaze again. "I want that, too. You and me. Together in love, and in life."

He kissed her again, and this time, he took her down to the bed, keeping them close. He wore only his jeans, and they felt sexy and rough against her thighs. They'd have to go—soon—but for now, she was reveling in the feel of him against her. His warm skin above, pressed against her, and the rough denim below. Delicious.

"I love everything about you, Syd," he whispered, breaking the kiss and working his way down her jaw to her neck. He nibbled and licked, kissed and teased, and she loved every moment of his passion and the sexy words he spoke as he smooched his way down her body. "You are the sexiest woman in the world and a power to be reckoned with. Do you know how much that turns me on?"

She reached downward to cup his hardness through the denim. "I think I have some idea," she teased him, squeezing gently as he groaned. She loved the deep sounds in his chest that reminded her a little of his dragon side. "You're incredibly sexy when you turn all dragon," she told him, reaching down to nip at his shoulder. "And you don't mind my flames, which is a huge bonus."

"Mind? *Draga*, sweetheart, I love that you burn as hot as I do," he assured her. "I've never been able to be fully myself with a woman. Do you know how freeing it is to be with you?"

She nodded, unable to speak as he paused to kiss her breasts, licking and rubbing his face against the soft skin that awaited his touch with eager anticipation. His cheeks were only a little rough—not enough to abrade her skin, but enough to let her feel the maleness of his jaw. So very exciting to her starved senses. She wanted to revel in his touch for hours, but her body was fast heating into a passionate uproar. She couldn't wait for hours. Probably not even for minutes. She needed him *now*.

She pushed at his jeans, taking a moment to work at the button that held them together then release the zipper. He didn't stop her. In fact, he lifted his hips to help as she pushed the fabric down, away from his skin. His briefs went with the jeans, and then, he was revealed. Hard. Hot. Strong. And all hers.

She reached for him, but he skittered away, moving her around instead. He placed her on her side as he faced her, then lifted her top thigh over his and made a place for himself between. She liked it. Especially when he slid into her, claiming his place.

They were face to face. Heart to heart. Skin to skin. Together.

Then, he began to move, and the motion was rhythmic...and wonderful. The motion was slow, learning, yearning. He was using the position to pace himself, she realized, and emotion burst in her heart as her body burned in flames of desire. He was doing this for her. Holding back when he didn't need to, out of care and...love.

"I love you, Paul," she told him, revealing her deepest heart to him as she gazed into his dark eyes. "I love you with all my heart."

He growled and flipped her onto her back driving deep as if he'd completely lost control. "I love you, too," he whispered urgently as he powered into her, driving her up the bed and up to new heights of passion. She loved making him wild. She'd have to look for ways to do it more often.

That was the last coherent thought she had as the world burst into shards of light and pleasure. She heard Paul growl her name as they both went over the cliff into pure, unadulterated bliss. He held her as she held him, and ecstasy rocked their world. A world they would share now, together. Forever.

Syd woke from a vision of the future so bright she had to catch her breath. She saw herself and Paul living the dream. Happy. Flying side by side through life, helping people where they could, fighting evil where they found it, and living in a most unexpected place. She knew it wasn't going to be all roses and daffodils. There would be hard days, but together, they could handle just about anything.

Though she would have to leave this house behind, better things were ahead. They would be able to stay in Phoenix for a little while longer, but she knew their next destination already.

"We have to go to Grizzly Cove," she said aloud, sensing Paul come awake beside her.

He leaned up on one elbow to look at her. "What?"

"You heard me." She smiled at him and reached one hand up to curl around his neck.

"But your family is here. Don't you want to spend time with them?" he asked.

"I do, and there will be time for that—a little now, and a lot later—but your family needs our help in Grizzly Cove. Not today or even tomorrow, but soon. We need to balance the water element with our fire and air. There's going to be a big fight with something in the ocean, and we need to be there for it. Your friends there are earth. We are both wind and fire. Right now, evil has the majority of the water, but not if we have anything to say about it." She narrowed her gaze as she made that statement.

"How did you...? Oh." His gaze sharpened as he looked deep into her eyes. "This is something you've seen?"

She nodded. "A very strong vision of our future." She smiled. "We'll have our ups and downs, but as long as we're together..." She felt tears of joy welling in her eyes and paused as she got a little choked up.

Paul dipped his head, kissing her tears away. "As long as we're together, we're going to be fantastic," he told her, finishing her thought in the best way possible. "I don't have to be clairvoyant to know that," he quipped, making her smile.

"Do you think your bear family will like me?" she asked, a hint of her uncertainty sounding in her voice.

"*Dragostea mea*, they're going to love you," he said, placing little kisses all over her face. "And you're going to love Grizzly Cove."

EPILOGUE

Things moved fast once the dragons started waking up and rejoining the world of men. Paul and Syd arranged for storage of her belongings after she packed up the things she most wanted with her. The problem of where they would stay in the interim was solved when Arthur called and relayed a message from Hans, inviting Paul and Syd to stay in the nest for a while, so Paul could get to know the other dragons, and vice versa.

Paul was so enthusiastic about the idea of spending time with other dragon shifters, Syd could hardly object. She wanted to spend time with Arthur, too. Her old friend had been hiding a big secret and she wanted a chance to talk with him about everything she had been learning in the past few days.

Syd stayed up top the next afternoon with Arthur, while Hans traveled with Paul back down to the nest in one of the tricked out mine carts. This trip downward was very different from the previous one. For one thing, there were dragons in both human and dragon form in each of the caverns along the way this time, and many more mine carts parked on side rails.

Paul hadn't noticed it before, but there were actually two sets of tracks running parallel to each other so that one cart could be going down into the nest while another was traveling upward. It was a two-way railroad system. In fact, as they entered one of the narrow tunnels about halfway through the journey, another cart passed by going upward. Hans waved as they passed, the carts going just slow enough so Paul could see the man and woman in the other cart before they were past.

"We're trying to stagger our presence up top for now," Hans told Paul as they continued moving downward. "There's a lot still to be done to secure the nest and we don't want to draw too much attention to ourselves before we're ready.

"Ready for what, exactly?" Paul asked, wondering yet again about the real reason behind the elaborate hideaway the dragon shifters had constructed centuries ago.

"War, Paul. I'm sorry to say." Hans's expression tightened. "This nest holds a dragon army. It was my task to gather our people and hide them. My job isn't entirely done yet, but soon I will pass the baton to my brother, who will see us to the next phase of preparedness. Then, when the time is right, the one who is destined to lead us all into battle will take command."

"Sounds like a complex plan," Paul mused, wondering how the dragons had known to prepare in such detail.

"It is," Hans agreed. "And yet, there are elements of uncertainty in it that we all must face." He nodded at Paul. "The dragon shifters gathered here have all pledged their allegiance to the Mother of All." He paused and his gaze was very direct. "Like you."

Paul was taken aback. "How can you know that?"

"Arthur confirmed it, but I knew already that he would never have let you into the mine without checking you out thoroughly. You had proved yourself to him already, and he has…abilities…I can only guess at. He is not just some crackpot old codger. He's a person of true power."

Paul nodded. "Yeah. I saw that for myself. He's a Knight of the Light."

"A *Chevalier?*" Hans seemed to think about it. "I can't say I'm surprised. He has that sort of aura about him. Not that I've known that many of his kind in my time, but I have crossed paths with one or two of his brethren in the distant past." Hans shrugged and changed the subject. "You and your mate are welcome to stay with us while we prepare. I would hope you might add your strength to our army."

"I'm not sure about that, unfortunately. My mate is a foreseer and she's already told me that we have to go back to my bear family in Grizzly Cove shortly. We are needed there to represent Wind and Fire. They are fighting a leviathan in the ocean, attempting to send it back where it belongs."

"A leviathan?" Hans seemed very interested. "The Destroyer was known to use such creatures. It is another sign that the time of battle nears. But, tell me more about this place, Grizzly Cove, and your family there. How is it that you have family among bears?"

For the rest of the journey down to the nest, Paul told Hans what he knew about the cove and how he'd come to be related to a Clan of Kamchatka bear shifters. Hans seemed greatly interested in the problems the bears had faced with the leviathan and Paul felt comfortable revealing what little he knew about the situation.

Eventually, they arrived and got out of the mine cart. A dark haired woman was waiting on the platform, tears in her eyes as she stepped forward.

"Paul, this is your aunt, Tilda Lebchenko. Your father's older sister. She was one of the last to wake since her resting place was at the far edges of the nest." Hans made the startling introduction, then faded into the background as Paul was completely blown away by the fact that the small woman in front of him was a blood relative.

He was going to ask if they were certain, but one look into her eyes let him know that she was family. It was like looking at a slightly skewed mirror. They had the same eyes. Same dark hair. Same pointed nose.

"You're..." He couldn't speak past the lump in his throat.

The woman stepped closer. "Forgive me, Paul. I didn't know my brother had mated, or that he'd had a son. I would never have joined the nest if I'd known." Her words sang healing to his wounded heart.

He wasn't sure which of them moved, but suddenly, she was in his arms and they were hugging and laughing and crying a little. It was a moment of joy and pain, sorrow and blistering hope for the future.

"Auntie Tilda," he whispered as he hugged her close. "I'm so happy to meet you."

Arthur and Syd had been on the very next rail car down and Syd felt tears welling in her eyes as she saw Paul hugging a woman who had to be related to him. Slightly older, she had the same exotic looks. Arthur had brought her down to the nest, much to her surprise, explaining that Hans had wanted to talk with Paul on the ride, but he'd requested that Syd be brought down as soon as possible.

Hans had known, Syd realized. He'd known Paul was about to meet family and he'd wanted her to be there for him. She didn't know much about Hans yet, but she was definitely beginning to like the guy.

"She is his father's sister," Arthur told Syd as they exited the mine cart. As soon as they were out, the cart parked itself on a side rail.

"An aunt," Syd breathed. "I'm so happy for him." Syd stood in the background, gripping Arthur's hand as they watched the reunion. She wouldn't intrude, but she would be there if he needed her.

"It is a privilege to witness such a happy moment," Arthur agreed and Syd realized the old shaman's dark eyes were glistening with emotion as well.

"You've been a great friend to me, Arthur," she told him quietly, squeezing his hand. "You managed to keep me in the dark about all this, but still, I know you've guided me like I think a father would have." She turned her head to meet his misty gaze. "If you don't mind...that's how I think of you. As a father figure. I never had one of my own, but if I could choose, I would choose you."

Arthur squeezed her hand in return. "And I would choose you as my daughter, Syd."

No more needed to be said on that subject. She'd said what she'd wanted to say for a long time and got back more in return than she'd ever expected. Now that she had some blood relatives in her life, she realized something even more important...

Blood might tie people together in the most basic way, but ultimately, some of the deepest ties could be formed by the heart, with people unrelated by blood, but bound by love. For all intents and purposes, Arthur had been her father since just after they'd met. He'd guided her like a father would. He'd helped her in subtle ways. She'd cared for him, as he had for her. He had a place in her heart that would never change.

She might have found a brother and a cousin and even a grandmother, but those relationships would take time to grow. In her mind and in her heart, she now understood that her relationship with Arthur was every bit as important as those blood ties. Some family, you were born to. Others, you chose. She was grateful for whatever benevolent deity had brought Arthur into her life and just as grateful, albeit in a different way, for Paul.

They would create a family together now—some of blood and some from those people they chose to adopt into their inner circle, and who chose them in return. She knew her life would never be lonely again. She and Paul would have a big circle that would only grow ever wider as they aged.

The future for them all looked very bright, indeed.

*

Deep under the Superstition Mountains, Hans surveyed his domain from the farthest edges of the fully awakened nest. When he'd read the signs of evil rising in the world again back in the 1700s, he'd devised this plan. Gather a hoard of riches to last into the coming centuries, and a group of like-minded kinsfolk to hide out together.

Dragon shifters had been hunted. Picked off one by one, at the time. A lone dragon had been easy pickings for bands of *Venifucus* mages, and they had done all they could to make dragon shifters extinct. But Hans had outsmarted them, and now, his friends and family were rising to fight another day.

The only problem they'd had over the centuries were the daring human treasure hunters who seemed to be constantly risking their lives to find gold in these treacherous mountains. He and his people had helped more than one prospector make it out alive, though their help had been unseen, for the most part.

Hans had even befriended of one of the prospectors back in the 1800s, and though he'd trusted Jacob, Hans's decision to give the man a little gold to make him go away had been a mistake in the long run. Who knew Jacob would die with more than twenty pounds of pure gold ore under his bed or speak cryptic clues about a gold mine hidden somewhere in the Superstition Mountains?

Hans shook his head. The Lost Dutchman had created more headaches for Hans and his people over the past century or so, but he couldn't regret helping the crafty German. Jacob had been smart enough to bring beer on his trips into the mountains, and Hans had enjoyed sitting with the fellow a few times and talking about the old country.

Jacob had spoken German, but Hans had been born in the Netherlands and had traveled widely before finding this remote part of the American Southwest. He'd been able to converse with Jacob in his native tongue, and they'd become friendly. It was Jacob, in fact, who had told Hans about Arthur, a local shaman who was reputed to be highly magical. Jacob's talkative ways had led Hans to secure Arthur's promise to guard the entry point they'd built—miles away from the actual nest.

After Jacob's accidental arrival to the nest, Hans and his friends had made sure such discoveries would never happen again. They'd sealed up the nearest entrance and created the railway and entrance far away from the heart of their domain. Then, Hans had made a deal with Arthur—who had turned out to be even more magical and powerful than Jacob knew—to act as gatekeeper.

It had been a good plan, but its time had come to an end with the rising of the phoenixes. Now, all bets were off, and it was time, once again, to fight.

Hans grinned as he looked at his army of dragons.

Those who served evil wouldn't know what was coming for them.

#

ABOUT THE AUTHOR

Bianca D'Arc has run a laboratory, climbed the corporate ladder in the shark-infested streets of lower Manhattan, studied and taught martial arts, and earned the right to put a whole bunch of letters after her name, but she's always enjoyed writing more than any of her other pursuits. She grew up and still lives on Long Island, where she keeps busy with an extensive garden, several aquariums full of very demanding fish, and writing her favorite genres of paranormal, fantasy and sci-fi romance.

Bianca loves to hear from readers and can be reached through Twitter (@BiancaDArc), Facebook (BiancaDArcAuthor) or through the various links on her website.

WELCOME TO THE D'ARC SIDE...
WWW.BIANCADARC.COM

OTHER BOOKS BY BIANCA D'ARC

WWW.BIANCADARC.COM